W9-AKU-023

Glimpses

A collection of
Nightrunner tales

Lynn
Flewelling

· NIGHTRUNNERS ·

Publisher: Three Crow Press
Editor and Owner: Reece Notley
www.threecrowpress.com

ISBN: 978 1453624913

Cover art by Anne Cain © 2010

First Published September 2010

The Collection: Glimpses contains the following:
Misfit © Lynn Flewelling
The Wild © Lynn Flewelling
By The River © Lynn Flewelling (previously published)
The Bond © Lynn Flewelling
Summer Players [Excerpt] © Lynn Flewelling

All illustrations included in this collection were
donated for use by the original artist who retains copyright.
Any duplications or reproductions are expressively
forbidden without prior consent of the artist.

The moral rights of the author and artists have been asserted.

All those characters in this publication, other than those clearly in the
public domain, are fictitious and any resemblance to real persons,
living or dead, is purely coincidental.

All rights reserved.

No part of this publication may be reproduced or transmitted in any
forms by any means, electronic or mechanical including
photocopying, recoding or any information retrieval system, without
prior permission, in writing, from the author or contributing artist.

The book is sold subject to the condition that it shall not, by way of
trade or otherwise, be lent, resold, hired out, or otherwise circulated
without the publisher's prior consent in any form of binding or cover
other than that in which it is published and without a similar
condition including this condition being imposed on the subsequent
purchaser.

Acknowledgements

Thanks first to Madame Editor, Reece Notley of Three Crows Press. Without her enthusiasm and expertise, this little book would not exist. Thanks also to my son Tim, for his editorial help, and to author Betty Blue for her advice on the naughty bits.

Glimpses

Lynn Flewelling

Table Of Contents

Table of Illustrations

The Bond

The Summer Players

Image Gallery

Praise for Lynn Flewelling

"Glimpses is full of treasures like Lynn Flewelling's deceptively easy and addictive storytelling, her vivid and engaging characters, and the amazing and heartfelt illustrations. I found it fascinating to see a younger, less outwardly confident Seregil in both 'Misfit' and 'By the River', and then to meet him in his much more worldly persona in the snippet of 'The Summer Players', the next Nightrunner novel. 'The Wild' is a poignant, brutal and uplifting tale of Alec's parents and his early childhood. While the deepening of Seregil and Alec's relationship in 'The Bond' is beautifully handled and is as emotionally satisfying for the reader as it is for the two friends and lovers. This book is a must have for fans of Lynn's Nightrunner books, and if you haven't started the series yet, then Glimpses will leave you eager to discover more about Seregil and Alec, their adventures and the unique and fantastical world that the pair inhabit."

—Suzanne McLeod, author of the Spellcrackers.com
urban fantasy series

"It's hard to imagine a lovelier gift to fans than this exquisite collection of gorgeously illustrated short stories. Flewelling indulges her loyal readers with these graceful glimpses 'between the lines' of the long-running and immensely popular Nightrunner series."

—Josh Lanyon, author of the Adrien English Mysteries
and the Holmes & Moriarity Mysteries

"An unmissable short story collection from Flewelling. Set in the Nightrunner universe Glimpses captures Flewelling's characters at formative moments in their various timelines. Some of the stories fill in details that I've been waiting on for years, others tell stories that I didn't know I wanted to know until I read them. And who can resist the story of how Seregil first met Micum Cavish, beloved if never a lover, or a glimpse at the young Phoria - before she turned so bitter. Illustrated by fans of the series it is fun to see how other readers envisage the characters."

—T.A. Moore, award-winning author of the Even Series

"Glimpses is a terrific collection, lovingly illustrated, a gift to all of us who love the Nightrunners. This rocks."
— *Patricia Briggs, New York Times Best-selling*
Author of the Mercy Thompson Series

"Magnificent, impressive … capture[s] some of the same flavor found in T. H. White's classic, The Once and Future King, as well as in Ursula Le Guin's Earthsea books. Factor in some essence of Mervyn Peake, and you have a winning combination."
— *Realms of Fantasy*

"Flewelling's Nightrunner books are popular among fantasy fans for a very simple reason—they're good."
— *Monroe (LA) News-Star*

"An intensely poignant tale that asks the question—how far should one go to change destiny? Lynn Flewelling delivers a tightly crafted narrative with vivid characters and a detailed background that quickly pulls the reader into her world."
— *Romantic Times*

"Memorable characters, an enthralling plot, and truly daunting evil.... The characters spring forth from the page not as well-crafted creations but as people.... The magic is refreshingly difficult, mysterious, and unpredictable. Lynn Flewelling has eschewed the easy shortcuts of clichéd minor characters and cookie-cutter backdrops to present a unique world.... I commend this one to your attention."
— *Robin Hobb, award-winning author of the The Realm*
of the Elderlings series and the Soldier Son Trilogy

"A splendid read, filled with magic, mystery, adventure, and taut suspense. Lynn Flewelling, bravo! Nicely done."
— *Dennis L. McKiernan*

Foreword

Many years ago, when I was still editing the Roc SF imprint, I cornered an agent friend of mine, waving a book in her face. "Why didn't you send me this author, when you were submitting it?"

She blanched a little. "Oh, but you already had [author redacted] on your list, so I thought it would be too similar."

"Argh," I growled. "I would have made room!"

So I lost out on my chance to be Lynn Flewelling's editor. But instead, I got to be her fan.

And that's a word I don't use easily: I've worked with many writers over the years, and I enjoy their work, I often love their work, but I don't often consider myself a fan So why Lynn Flewelling? Because when I start one of her stories, I know that I'll lose the rest of the day to anything else. Period. She writes of people I care about, adventures that I can lose myself in, and, underneath it all she writes about things that matter. About love and friendship. Loyalty and fear. The many layers of faith, and the equal layers of betrayal. And she does it without losing sight of the most important, cannot-be-underestimated elements of writing: Make It Fun. Even if you're tearing your readers' hearts out, make them enjoy it.

Lynn is heterosexual. In case anyone was wondering. So the fact that her main characters in the Nightrunner series are gay could have backfired, could have been seen as a ploy to ride a particular subgenre bandwagon, except for the fact that Seregil and Alec are characters formed by their experiences, rather than formed to BE their experiences. When Lynn writes about gender issues, ostracism and the difficulties of knowing and accepting not only who you are, but who you love, readers—no matter what their self-identifications, can find their own emotions and personal conflicts there.

That's a gift. That's storytelling.

I've been doubly fortunate, since that first encounter with *Luck In The Shadows*, to also be able to claim Lynn as a friend. For those of you who know that her totem animal is the otter, I can confirm, that yes, she shares many traits with that animal—she's friendly, open, inquisitive, and cracks shells open with rocks.

Oh no, wait...

There are many stories I could tell, from the years of rooming together at conventions, of sitting long over drinks, and of sharing tea—one of Lynn's obsessions, as she tries to wean me from my beloved coffee—but then she would probably and rightfully kill me.

So I will say only that it has been my pleasure, for the past fourteen years, to watch Lynn's readership grow, from those of us who knew early on, to people discovering her work only now. And it is my great pleasure to introduce you to this collection, which brings us into the heart of her world and her characters, and does what Lynn does best: makes us care.

Laura Anne Gilman
September, 2010

A Few Words

Dear Reader, what you hold in your hands is a small collection of stories that fill in a few gaps in the Nightrunner world's history, little glimpses people have asked for over the years.

This all began in 2001 when, for reasons I don't recall, I wrote a short story called "*By the River*," in which Seregil and Micum Cavish meet for the first time, many years before the Nightrunner Series begins. It was fun; I'd never really considered the details before. I wrote it for my own amusement, then shared it online with several fan groups.

Since then, readers have requested other stories, most particularly an account of Seregil and Alec's first night as lovers. That appears here as "*The Bond*," the first Nightrunner erotica I have ever written. It takes place at the end of *Stalking Darkness*, the summer after the death of Seregil's beloved mentor, the wizard Nysander and opens just after Seregil, wracked with guilt, tries to leave everyone behind.

"*Misfit*" is two stories in one: the events leading up to Seregil becoming Nysander's apprentice soon after his exile from Aurënen, his native country, and his first Skalan sexual liaison. This story also contains homoerotic scenes.

"*The Wild*," also a two-in-one, reveals a bit of Alec's early childhood with his father, Amasa, and how his parents met.

Finally, a snippet from my forthcoming Nightrunner novel, *The Summer Players*. At least that's what it's called at the moment. Look for it in 2011 from Spectra.

You will also find illustrations with each story. Since the earliest days of the Nightrunner series, people have sent me artwork inspired by my stories. I treasure every one of them, as I know each is a labor of love. After all these years, it still thrills me that people do things like that. So it only seemed right that this book be illustrated by fans.

I hope you enjoy these pictures as much as I do. I received many more than I could possibly use, and it was very difficult narrowing the choices down to the few that fit here, but as I said, every one I received is appreciated.

I hope you enjoy these little glimpses.

Lynn Flewelling
Redlands, California
September, 2010

Come with me and learn to steal things!

OK!

THE END

Misfit

Nysander hummed softly to himself as he walked through the gloomy palace corridors. A few of the courtiers he passed cast him a questioning glance, but most gave him a smile or respectful nod, used to his quirks. His little tricks at the royal banquet last night— making rings from gold coins, casting a rain of flowers, and sending empty platters floating back to the kitchen—had gone over well, as usual. People tended to assume that this was why the queen favored him. That suited the old wizard just fine.

He was well acquainted with Idrilain's suite of rooms, having visited four queens before her here. He'd known Idrilain from birth and both loved and respected the warrior ruler she'd become.

It was a pleasant autumn day and he found her and her women sitting in her sunny courtyard, together with her second daughter, young Aralain. The sun glittered on pale blonde hair as she and her mother looked up and smiled at Nysander.

"Ah, here you are, my friend! Welcome back." The queen rose to take his hands. "Four months is too long not to see you. How was your journey?"

"Very pleasant, my dear." They dispensed with titles in private. "The island is very nice this time of year."

"I miss it," Idrilain said with a sigh. "I want to hear all about it, and how Rabinis is faring, but first there's someone I'd like you to meet. Kallia, summon Seregil."

One of the younger ladies-in-waiting went inside.

"Seregil?" asked Nysander. "An Aurënfaie?"

"Yes. A distant kinsman of mine. He arrived just after you left. I've recently placed him with Emidas."

"Indeed?" Emidas was the queen's chief scribe. While it was an honorable post, it seemed an odd choice for a kinsman.

"I'm afraid he's having trouble adjusting to court life. I made him a page first, but he was a bit old, and wasn't really suited to the position."

"How so?"

Idrilain gave him a wry look. "He had a habit of not being where he was supposed to."

Nysander chuckled at that. "Ah, I see."

"But he's well educated and writes with a very fine hand. Emidas has been happy with him so far. Well, mostly. Seregil is a bit headstrong, and apparently gets bored easily."

Nysander could well imagine, having traveled in Aurënen. The 'faie had no royalty, and nothing so formal as the Skalan court.

The young woman soon returned with a pretty youth. His ink-stained fingers and short green robe marked him as a junior scribe. He had the fine features of a pure 'faie, framed by long dark brown hair loose over his shoulders. His grey eyes betrayed a deep sadness even as he gave Nysander a stiff bow and a forced smile. He looked to be about eighteen in human years.

Nysander took all that in at a glance, but it wasn't what most caught his attention; the young 'faie had magic in him. Nysander could just make out the faint aura of it around him. It was a shame to waste him as a minor functionary. If he'd been here when the young man had arrived he might have requested him for the Orëska.

2

"Nysander, this is my kinsman Seregil," said Idrilain. "Seregil, this is Lord Nysander í Azusthra, one of the chief wizards of the Orëska House and a great friend of mine."

"My lord, I am very honored to meet you," said Seregil. His Skalan was cultured and carried the lilt of a western clan. Oddly, Idrilain hadn't used Seregil's formal name, with its string of patronymics and clan.

"Can Seregil take tea with us, Mother?" asked Aralain, and Nysander guessed that she was a bit smitten with the young man.

Idrilain smiled. "I'm sure his master can spare him for a little while."

Seregil bowed again and joined the them at a small tea table by the fountain.

"Well, you are a long way from home, my boy," said Nysander. "How are you enjoying Rhíminee so far?"

"I haven't seen much beyond the palace, my lord. But it's very pleasant here."

Nysander could tell he didn't mean a word of it. Though he still smiled politely, it was clear that Seregil wasn't here by his own choice. As much as Nysander wanted to ask him more about himself, he sensed that it wouldn't be welcome and to brush his thoughts would be rude.

The way Seregil spoke—when he did speak—and the genteel manner in which he handled his delicate porcelain tea bowl all reinforced Nysander's initial impression that he was from a cultured, perhaps sheltered background. What in the world was he doing here?

Just then they heard raised voices and Phoria's two older children burst in. At eighteen, Princess Phoria and her twin, Prince Korathan, were fair and tall like their mother. Phoria was slender, while Korathan had a lean athlete's build.

"Mother, Phoria won't let me ride Bright Star!" Korathan exclaimed.

"Because he'll break her neck if he tries," Phoria retorted. "Oh, hello, Nysander! And Seregil! It's good to see you."

"Cousin," Korathan said, acknowledging Seregil, as well.

"Your Highnesses." A genuine smile transformed Seregil before Nysander's eyes. He was more than pretty; he was quite beautiful, perhaps more than was good for him here at court. At least he'd made friends with the queen's children. No doubt he'd rather have been with them than sitting here in his stiff collared robe.

Seregil did his best to concentrate on the document in front of him, a manifest from a grain shipment. The scriptorium was silent except for the light scratch of quills on parchment and the occasional distant honking of the Vs of wild geese flying over the city. Outside in the garden, new fallen snow sparkled in the sun under a clear blue sky. Despite the cold draft from the window casement beside him, he longed to be out there, not in this dreary chamber with its bare walls and cold stone floor. His desk was at the back of the room, furthest from the great hearth. He and the other junior scribes worked with their cloaks on.

He'd been at this kind of work for almost three months now and he was heartily sick of it. The manifest he was copying out was the sort of task Emidas thought him worthy of, or perhaps it was spite. Seregil knew he'd been foisted on the head scribe after he'd failed as a page. Well, he hadn't failed so much as not cared. The whole artifice of the Skalan royal court, all that bowing and scraping and memorizing of titles grated on his nerves. And it was boring. And these clothes!

He hadn't known what boredom was, though, until they stuck him here with a score of men and women who never lifted their noses from their task. Lord Emidas carried a short walking stick with a knob on the end and wasn't above rapping the head or shoulder of any slackers. Seregil had found that out the first day and nearly punched the man. No one had ever laid hands on him like that. No one touched the Khirnari's son—

Except that I'm not, anymore.

"Seregil, come here, please," Emidas called from his high desk at the front of the room, where he'd been checking through the day's work. Seregil felt a little spark of hope.

He felt the eyes of the others on him as he passed them on his way to the front of the room.

"What is this?" Emidas asked, holding up the manifest for a shipment of armor Seregil had completed yesterday. He'd done it in the form of an illuminated manuscript, with dragons, sea serpents and griffons intertwined with the fancy capital letters at the beginning of each paragraph. He done it partly out of boredom, and partly in the hope that Emidas would give him something more interesting to work on.

"I thought, maybe—"

"You thought you could impress me by wasting time creating something utterly useless?"

Seregil clenched his fists inside his sleeves. It was good work, as good as anything he'd seen here.

"It does show some promise," the man sniffed. "Perhaps in a year or two, when you've mastered the basics, I will consider instructing you in the more elaborate styles." He handed it back to Seregil. "Please copy this over in the proper form. Immediately."

"But I'm in the middle of that field report. Duke Nirus needs it today."

"Well then, you'd better get started."

A year? Two? Seregil swallowed his anger and hurt as he walked back down the long aisle to his desk. Everyone in the room must have heard. He caught a few smirking down at their parchments as he passed and someone snickered. Pimple-faced Baleus, no doubt. Not that he was the only one who liked to see Seregil taken down a peg. Being known to be queen's kin hadn't done him much good.

Probably his miserable attitude hadn't, either. Sometimes he regretted getting off on the wrong foot with just about everyone. He hadn't been like this—before.

The extra work kept him in the scriptorium long after night had fallen and everyone else went off to supper, leaving him at his desk with a single lamp to work by. He moved to a desk closer to the fire, but it was dying and the day's supply of wood was gone. Shivering made his script a little crooked, but at this point he didn't give a damn.

A *year* before Emidas let him do anything he was capable of? He'd go mad!

His fingers were cramping with cold when he finally put the manifest on Emidas' desk, tucked the field report in a leather folio with the queen's crest on it, and blew out the lamp.

It was a long walk to the duke's private chambers on the far side of the palace, he thought glumly, feeling his way toward the door. He'd be lucky to find any supper now. He'd probably just go back to his room. Alone.

He used to love this time of day—supper with his sprawling extended family at the clan house, then music or out for nighttime games with Kheeta and their friends. Or those summer trysts with Ilar ...

He paused by the door in the darkened room, one hand braced against the wall as pain flared in his heart. *Don't think of home, not any of it! Don't think of* him!

But it was too late. Grief and loneliness and shame rolled over him in a suffocating wave. He slid to the floor, tears he couldn't hold back dripping onto the folio clutched in his hands.

"Damn it!" He hadn't cried since he came here.

At times like this, which came all too frequently lately, he regretted that he hadn't loaded his pockets with ballast stones and thrown himself off the ship that carried him into exile when he'd had the chance. But he knew how to tie a noose. Or he could find some high place and jump. Or open a vein in a warm bath. That last one held the most appeal.

As he knelt there, feeling very sorry for himself, he heard footsteps approaching. Before he could collect himself the door swung inward and struck his shoulder.

"Seregil?"

It was Prince Korathan, the last person Seregil wanted to see him in this pathetic state. Caught in the light of the open doorway, he wiped his face hastily on his sleeve and stood up.

Korathan had a mug of ale in one hand and a meat pasty in a napkin in the other. "What's wrong? Why are you here in the dark?"

Seregil held up the folio. "I just finished. I have to deliver this to Duke Nirus. What are you doing here?" The words came out much harsher than he'd intended.

But Korathan just smiled. "I heard Emidas kept you late again, so I brought you some supper."

He put the mug and the pasty down on a desk, then took a lamp and lit it from one in the corridor. "Go on and eat," he urged, shutting the door again. "Then I'll walk with you to the duke's rooms."

"Thank you." It was hard to speak with a lump in your throat. Korathan and his sisters were really the only friends he had in this wretched place, and he seldom got to see them. The queen was kind and the princesses were pleasant, but only the prince sought him out.

He knew Korathan must have seen that he'd been crying, but the prince didn't say anything. Seregil deeply appreciated that. Instead, Korathan talked about a new horse his father had given him while Seregil ate. Between the food and the companionship, Seregil began to feel a little better.

"Say, after we get those papers delivered, we could go back to my rooms and play some bakshi," Korathan offered. "You've almost got the hang of it."

Seregil managed a smile. "You're a good teacher."

When he was finished eating, he blew out the lamp again and they set off together. There were still many nobles strolling the halls and they all bowed respectfully to the prince, who mostly ignored them as he told Seregil more about the strategy of the game. Seregil got a few curious looks, as he always did. He'd heard there were other 'faie in the city, but he was the only one in the palace, and a bit of a mystery. Or perhaps it was seeing the prince with a lowly junior scribe. Still, with Korathan beside him, Seregil didn't feel so lonely and out of place.

The scriptorium was in a wing of the sprawling palace reserved for various functionaries like Emidas. After several twists and turns, however, they entered the palace proper, where there were tapestries on the walls and carpets on the floor. These did little soften the dour ugliness of the place, to Seregil's eye.

"I know a short cut," Korathan said, taking him by the hand and leading him out into a very large, dark garden. The pathways had been cleared, but snow lay deep on either side.

As they headed for a lighted doorway on the far side, Korathan didn't let go of Seregil's hand. He was wearing a wool surcoat and boots. Seregil was shivering in his cloak and slippers. It was a long way across this garden.

"You're cold. I'm sorry. Maybe we shouldn't have come this way." Korathan stopped and put an arm around Seregil's shoulders. "Is that better?"

"That's all right. We're almost there." Seregil started to walk but Korathan's arm tightened around his shoulders, holding him fast.

Then the one-armed embrace became a two-armed hug. "You're miserable here, aren't you?"

In all the time Seregil had been here, no one had ever asked him that. Or hugged him. A feeling very akin to relief welled up in his heart, and he nodded as he hugged

him back.

Korathan stroked Seregil's hair, then kissed him gently on the forehead. "I'll speak to Mother."

"Thank you!"

Korathan looked down at him for a moment, the kissed him on the lips. It lasted too long for a family kiss. Seregil froze, not knowing what to do.

"Why did you do that?" he asked when Korathan was finished.

"You didn't like it?"

"I—uh—" Korathan's arms were still around him but he released Seregil when he stepped back to collect his thoughts. "I didn't know that you liked men."

"I heard you do."

Seregil had guessed there might be rumors about him, but not that. Then again, the queen knew the whole sordid story. Maybe she'd told Korathan? "What else did you hear?" he demanded, angry now.

"Just that you're here because of something that happened with a lover. I'm sorry, I shouldn't have presumed—"

"Is that all you heard?"

"Yes! Seregil, I'm sorry. It's just that you look so sad all the time."

Seregil pushed past him and started back the way they'd come. "I don't need your pity!"

"It's not pity!" Korathan called after him. "I like you."

The words, and the sincerity with which they were spoken surprised Seregil in equal measure. Turning, he looked back at the prince, who was standing where Seregil had left him.

"I like you," Korathan said again. "And I'm sorry I kissed you. Please, let's play bakshi, like we planned."

Seregil wavered a moment as memories of betrayal threatened to overwhelm him again. At least Korathan hadn't claimed he loved him. Seregil would have kept walking if he had. Instead, he went back to Korathan and fell silently into step beside him as they continued through the garden.

The prince's fine suite of rooms was just down the corridor from the queen's, and opulently furnished. There was a large main sitting room and a bedroom beyond. The sofa and armchairs were soft leather, and there were hunting trophies and murals of hunting scenes covering the walls. A fire crackled in the ornate marble fireplace. They moved the bakshi table and two chairs in front of the fire and Korathan sent a servant for wine.

Settling at the board, Korathan took out his leather bag of stones, and another one like it, which he handed to Seregil. "A gift, cousin."

Seregil opened it and found a collection of gaming stones made of blood red carnelian. They bore an incised design of fighting dragons. "Thank you! They're beautiful."

"I thought of you when I saw them. Dragons for Aura and Illior?"

"Don't say that," Seregil said with a smile. "They're fighting. I'll just think of them as real ones."

"Have you seen real ones?"

"They're common as sparrows in the mountains." Somehow it didn't hurt, talking about home with him.

They drank wine and played game after game. Korathan made Seregil laugh, and made him feel welcome. Only when he was with Korathan did he ever really enjoy himself.

They continued to play and talk and laugh until the candles burned down almost to the sockets. Seregil finally won a game, and in only a few moves, too.

"Excellent! I think you're ready for the gambling houses," Korathan told him. "It will do you good to get out of this place."

"I'd like that." Seregil yawned and looked around at the guttering candles. "It's late. I should be going."

"It's a long way back to that kennel of a room they have you in. Stay here tonight, why don't you? We can have another game."

That certainly was better than going out into those long, cold corridors, and the wine had made him a little dizzy. "All right. Thanks."

They cleared the board and started another round. Seregil thought again how comfortable he felt with Korathan, and grateful.

Being around him made life in this strange land bearable. He felt he owed him something for that.

As Korathan was concentrating on his next move, Seregil blurted out, "It's all right that you kissed me. I—I don't mind."

Korathan looked up at him in surprise. "I'm glad. I was afraid I'd hurt your feelings."

"No, I was just startled."

Korathan smiled as he pushed a piece across the board, blunting the spear Seregil had been building. "Then I'll give you better warning the next time."

"Next time?"

"If you want there to be a next time," Korathan replied. "I really do like you, Seregil."

Seregil's cheeks went hot. Korathan wanted to kiss him again, and right now that didn't seem such a bad idea. It felt like a lifetime ago since Ilar had. That thought hurt.

"There's that sadness," said Korathan. "Do I need to apologize again?"

Seregil slowly shook his head. "No, you don't. I think I'd like that."

Korathan immediately took him up on the offer. Standing, he pulled Seregil to his feet and took him in his arms for a long, intense kiss that left Seregil a little unsteady. Taking Korathan's face between his hands as Ilar used to do with him, Seregil kissed him back. He could feel Korathan's cock hard through their clothes, next to his own. Reaching between them, he stroked Korathan's erection. The prince let out a low groan and did the same for him with far more skill than Seregil possessed. He had Seregil panting in an instant.

Korathan smiled down at him. "I think you want more than kissing."

Seregil managed a nod. Korathan unbuttoned Seregil's coat and eased it off his shoulders, letting it fall to the floor. Seregil undid the lacings of his shirt and pulled it over his head.

Korathan took off his own coat and shirt, then kissed him again. His body was warm and hard against Seregil's. It felt good. So good that he didn't mind at all when they somehow ended up naked on Korathan's big bed. He'd never been completely naked with Ilar and found himself caught between excitement and embarrassment. His own pale body looked so scrawny next to Korathan's lean muscle. But Korathan soon overwhelmed any hesitancy, kissing him and touching him all over. Seregil gasped as the prince nipped his neck just to the point of pain. It immediately turned to pleasure again as Korathan swirled his hot tongue around Seregil's left nipple. He ran his hard, sword-callused hands down Seregil's sides to grip his hips for a moment, then caressed the insides of each thigh with fingers and lips.

Seregil's whole body was consumed with heat, both by the feeling of being touched so intimately, but also the sight of the handsome young man doing the touching. Korathan knelt beside him, pale hair hanging down around his face to tickle as he kissed Seregil's belly. When Seregil tried to do the same for him, however, Korathan laughed and pushed him down on the bed again, then wrapped his hand around Seregil's cock and stroked him until Seregil was moaning between clenched teeth. Just as he was about to come in Korathan's hand, however, the prince stopped and stretched out close beside Seregil, kissing him and running his fingers through Seregil's tangled hair. "You're very beautiful, you know."

"No—"

"Yes, you are, and you know it," Korathan teased, stroking Seregil's belly just beyond reach of his cock.

"Please!" Seregil groaned, shivering with raw sensation.

But Korathan continued to tease him until Seregil could hardly stand the intensity of the feelings coursing through every fiber of his being. He'd never been more aroused in his life. At last Korathan kissed his way down the length of Seregil's shaft, licked at the bead of honey that had formed there, then took Seregil's cock firmly in his fist again and quickly brought him to a long and blinding climax that left Seregil feeling like he was floating several inches above the bed.

Before he could gather his wits enough to thank Korathan, the prince rolled Seregil over onto his side and spooned in behind him, gently fondling his softening cock. Korathan's was still very hard and hot against Seregil's backside.

Nuzzling Seregil's ear, Korathan slid his hand back to cup Seregil buttock and whispered, "Have you ever had a man here?"

"No ... " Seregil knew what he meant, though. Male unions were not uncommon in Aurënen and people talked. Ilar had even hinted at it, though they'd never gotten that far. "I hear it hurts."

"Just a little, at the start, then it feels very good." Korathan licked Seregil's ear and squeezed his bottom again. "I'd be honored to be the first."

Still awash in pleasurable sensations from all that Korathan had done to him so far, and glowing with wine, Seregil nodded slowly. "I suppose we could try."

They made love often after that, but always in secret. It was Korathan's wish, and Seregil was happy not to give anyone more reason to gossip about him.

Korathan was rougher with him than Ilar had been, but it was only passion and Seregil didn't mind. Not at all, even on the nights when Korathan kept him until dawn, making Seregil late for work. Once there, Seregil had a hard time not thinking about him during the day—Korathan's hand tight and merciless around Seregil's cock as he rocked against him, into him, nipping his neck and shoulders...

This sort of wool gathering earned Seregil more frequent thumps from Emidas's stick.

He was later than usual one morning near the end of winter, having had to fetch a heavy, crumbling tome from the palace library to be copied over. He'd forgotten to do it yesterday in his haste to meet Korathan.

For once he was excited about an assignment. The book was very old and fragile, and had illuminated capitals at the head of each chapter. He was quite proud that Emidas had entrusted it to him and anxious to escape the monotony of manifests and letters.

Seregil was relieved to see that Emidas wasn't at his desk yet. As he started for his own, however, someone pointed at him and laughed. He tried to ignore it, but soon most of the room was laughing and talking behind their hands.

"What?" Seregil demanded.

"Nice love bites on your neck, Master Seregil," Amidas snickered from across the aisle.

Seregil blushed hotly, which only drew more laughter. He always tried to be careful, and not let Korathan mark him anywhere that showed, but the prince had been more ardent than usual last night. There must be something showing above his collar.

If they knew who my lover was, they wouldn't be laughing in my face, he thought angrily and had to resist the urge to blurt out the truth.

As it was, he had no choice but to continue on down the aisle and hope they'd lose interest soon. Just as he reached his desk, however, his chief nemesis, Baleus, said loud enough for everyone to hear, "I bet he paid you well. I hear 'faie tail doesn't come cheaply!"

The sheer magnitude of the insult stunned Seregil. An exile he might be, but in this benighted land he still had some honor. Lacking a sword, he hit Baleus over the head with the book as hard as he could. The fragile volume fell to pieces in his hands, pages fluttering down around the two of them.

"You little bastard!" Baleus staggered up and swung his fist at Seregil.

Seregil dodged the clumsy blow but couldn't escape this second, vile accusation. As he raised his fist, however, someone caught his arm and yanked him away.

Seregil pulled free and found himself facing a furious Emidas.

"Stop, the pair of you! What is the meaning of this?" the scribe demanded, glaring at both of them and the scattered remains of the book.

"He called me a whore, *and* a bastard!" Seregil told him.

"Is that all?" Emidas regarded him in disbelief, then slapped him across the face. "For that you destroyed a three hundred-year-old book?"

"Is that *all*?" Seregil gasped as more laughter broke out. The words hurt far more than the slap. Knowing better than to strike Emidas, Seregil instead snatched up an inkwell and emptied it over the man's head, then snarled in his face, "You have no honor! Not one of you!"

Shoving Emidas out of the way, Seregil stalked off for the door, pulling off his scribe's robe as he went.

"The queen will hear of this!" Emidas shouted after him.

Seregil tossed the robe on the floor as he went out. "Yes, she will!"

And so would Korathan.

Research had kept Nysander busy in his tower for most of the winter. Being without an apprentice at the moment, he had to do everything himself, but he didn't mind. As much as he missed Alia, he was happy that she'd found a place with a noble household. She wrote him regularly of her progress, as did his other former students.

The tower was a bit empty without her, he had to admit, but he wasn't about to take on just anyone. A poorly chosen apprentice was nothing but a nuisance and a burden. His thoughts turned once again to the lonely Aurënfaie.

Given the close ties between the Orëska and the court, it was only natural that gossip should flow back and forth and Nysander had always found it useful to pay attention. Now and then one learned something of use.

It was his friend Magyana who brought him word of Seregil.

"I was just over at the palace," the old wizard told him over tea. "It seems that young Aurënfaie has been dismissed from another post."

"What for this time?"

"Apparently he attacked another scribe, and Lord Emidas himself."

"Indeed?" Unhappiness such as he'd sensed in the young 'faie eventually found some outlet. "What were the circumstances?"

"I don't know, but Seregil's with the household guard now. Word is he's quite the swordsman. Perhaps this will suit him better."

Nysander sighed. Another missed opportunity.

Magyana refilled her cup from the old brown teapot. "I heard something else of him, as well. Or rather, overheard it from the servants."

"Oh? And what would that be?"

"That young Seregil is Prince Korathan's current lover."

Nysander raised an eyebrow at that. "I see. I wonder if that is a good idea?" Korathan was known not to stay with anyone for long.

"There was some debate as to who seduced whom."

Nysander thought of the unhappy young man he'd met. There had been an air of innocence about him, or so Nysander had thought.

"My money is on the prince," Magyana said dryly.

Nysander shrugged. "Well, it's no concern of mine, but I wonder how it will end?"

Spring rain lashed against the bed chamber windows as Korathan tumbled Seregil onto the bed and stretched out on top of him. "I missed you! Three nights is too long. I don't think I like this new post of yours."

Seregil wrapped his arms around his tall lover, inhaling his rich scent. "Then you shouldn't have gotten it for me, should you?"

"But you're happier with the guard?"

"Yes!" Seregil kissed him soundly and grinned up at him. "I'd almost forgotten the feeling of a sword in my hand."

"Really?" Korathan pulled Seregil's hand to his cock and had him wrap his fingers around it. "Not much different, is it?"

Seregil laughed and took advantage of their position, rocking his hips to rub their two erections together and pulling a sigh of pleasure from his lover. He loved Korathan's body, loved knowing what do to do make him hard, make him come ... And Korathan could play Seregil's body like a harp.

The prince wasted little time on foreplay tonight. Making use of the flask of oil he kept beside the bed, he prepared them both, then gripped Seregil by the hips and plunged in. Seregil hissed at the brief pain, but as Korathan had promised him that first night together, it only lasted a moment and was well worth the pleasure that followed, especially when Korathan wrapped his hand around Seregil's shaft and pumped him in time to his thrusts. Heat blossomed through Seregil's body as he leaned back against Korathan, moving in perfect unison.

So lost in pleasure were they that neither one heard Phoria enter the sitting room, didn't even know she was there until she appeared in the open bedroom doorway.

"What in Bilairy's name—?" She was paler than usual and looking at them aghast. "Seregil! How could you?"

"Damn it, sister!" Korathan pushed Seregil away and pulled the corner of the comforter over the two of them.

"Get out!" Phoria growled.

Seregil knew she was speaking to him. He looked to Korathan to defend him, but the prince just murmured, "You'd best go."

Shocked, mortified, and deeply hurt, Seregil struggled off the bed, grabbed what he could of his scattered clothing and hurried past her. She slammed the door after him and he could hear her shouting at her brother. Yanking on his breeches and shirt, he was almost out the door and free before he caught the word "whore."

Barefoot and coatless, he ignored the looks he got from servants as he ran back to his room and shut the door. Fighting back angry tears, he collapsed into a chair by the window and waited for Korathan to come explain himself.

But the night passed and Korathan never came.

Nysander had forgotten all about Seregil again, until word came in early spring that he was in disgrace, dismissed from his post with the household guard, though no one seemed to know why.

It was raining as Nysander as set off for the palace, and the bleak color of the sky reminded him of the Seregil's eyes the day they'd met. At the palace the wizard was directed to the family wing, though to the end of it furthest from the royal quarters. A young page led him through several passages to the archway that led to the south garden.

"He's out there, my lord," the page told him. "I tried to make him come in, but he won't."

The rain was coming down even harder now, and he could just make out someone wrapped in a dark mantle hunched on one of the marble benches. Nysander dismissed the page, then pulled up the hood of his cloak and walked out to join the young man.

Seregil ignored Nysander until the wizard sat down beside him and said in Aurënfaie, "Hello again, young Seregil."

"Who—" Seregil turned to look at him with what appeared to be annoyance, but his expression changed to one of respect when he realized to whom he was speaking. His face was thinner than Nysander remembered and his mantle was soaked through. Nysander couldn't tell if it was rain on his cheeks, or tears. "Hello, Lord Nysander."

Nysander was impressed. He'd seen Seregil at banquets, and now and then with Prince Korathan, but they'd spoken only once and briefly.

He cast a shelter spell to keep off the rain. "This is not a very pleasant place you've chosen. But perhaps it suits your mood?"

"I suppose it does, my lord."

"I take it you are not very happy here in Rhíminee."

Seregil shrugged.

"You are wasted here at the palace, you know. What post do you hold now?"

"None, thanks to that bitch Phoria!" Seregil replied bitterly.

"That's no way to refer to the Princess Royal, especially here," Nysander cautioned. This one had spirit, at least.

"What will they do? Cut off my head? Lock me in their Red Tower? That's fine with me. Anything would be better than staying another day in this miserable place!"

Nysander suppressed a smile at the childish outburst. "I see. Well, then perhaps you would like to come have tea with me at the Orëska House. Look, you can just see the towers from here, above those roofs. The one on the right is mine. Really now, I think you are in need of some dry clothes, too. In fact, given how you are shivering, I think we should get you inside at once."

Seregil let out a humorless laugh. "I don't have a horse."

"You do not need one, dear boy. I am a wizard, after all."

He made a cage with his fingers and summoned the translocation spell. It began with a tiny speck of darkness, but as he opened his hands and spread his arms, it expanded to a black, spinning disk large enough for a man to step through, which was its purpose.

"What is that?" Seregil exclaimed, leaning closer to see.

"A quicker way back to my rooms." Nysander held out his hand. "You should hang onto me this first time."

He was surprised at how readily Seregil did so. The magic clearly interested him. The lack of fear was also encouraging.

"Stand close to me and step in. It is just like going through a doorway."

Holding onto Nysander's sleeve, Seregil stepped into the darkness with him.

It truly was like simply walking into another room—Nysander's casting room in this case—but as he emerged he found Seregil on his hands and knees, vomiting violently on the polished stone floor. Nysander was glad he hadn't taken them to his sitting room; he'd have ruined the carpet.

"What—what did—do to—me?" Seregil demanded between heaves. Nothing was coming up now, but he was still retching.

"Nothing, I assure you!" Nysander said, cleaning up the mess with a spell. He'd never seen anyone react this way before.

Seregil got to his feet with Nysander's help and staggered out into the main work room. Once there he stopped and gazed around with his mouth open, taking in the towering stacks of manuscripts around the room, and the crucibles, books, and general clutter covering the work benches. The polished brass astrolabe on the mezzanine above glinted dully in the grey light coming down through the round glass dome that capped the tower. "You *live* here?"

"I work here. I live downstairs. Come along."

Holding Seregil by the elbow, Nysander got him downstairs to Alia's old room. He found a blue-and-white apprentice robe in one of the clothes chests and gave it to him. Seregil took it with shaking hands and looked down at it as if he couldn't fathom what it was. It appeared he was still a little dazed.

"Put it on, dear boy. Leave your clothing here for the servant and come to the room across the hall when you are ready."

Nysander went out and closed the door to give him privacy, then walked across the corridor to the sitting room. The servant had stacked wood and kindling in the fireplace. He tossed in a fire chip and flames quickly licked up.

Seregil came in a few minutes latter, dressed in the robe, his wet hair looking as if he'd tried to comb it into some order with his fingers. The soft robe had been Saren's and was too big on him, but at least it was dry and warm. Seregil was still shivering, so Nysander guided him to one of the armchairs in front of the fire and spread a lap robe over Seregil's knees.

"Better now?" he asked, swinging the kettle on its iron hook over the flames to heat.

"Yes, thank you." Seregil pulled his knees up against his chest, and wrapped his arms around them, looking very much younger in his oversized robe, bare toes just visible below its hem, curled over the edge of the armchair. "So, you use magic to stop the rain, go from here to there, and clean up your floor, but you make the tea yourself?"

"Yes. It comes out much better that way." Nysander settled in the chair across the hearth. "Magic has its place, but not for everything. Besides, I enjoy it."

"Oh."

They sat there in awkward silence for a few moments, but soon Seregil was looking around the room with apparent interest. That was odd.

"What do you think of my mural?" the wizard asked.

Seregil glanced at the thin band of paintings that ringed the room. It possessed more than a minor magic; it was the room's chief defense. Seregil should have been mesmerized by it by now.

"It's pretty," Seregil replied. "Whoever painted those dragons must have seen a real one. They're better than anything I saw at the palace."

Nothing. No effect at all. Nysander had never seen this before. That, and the way the translocation had sickened Seregil were most interesting.

"Tell me, Seregil, have you had any training in magic?"

"Me?" Seregil gave another of those humorless laughs. "I'm no wizard."

"That is very odd, my young friend, because you do have some ability. I saw it in you the first time we met."

"With all respect, my lord, you're wrong."

Nysander let that go for now. "Do you know any wizards in your land?"

"A few." The mention of his homeland drove the smile from his face, which only increased Nysander's curiosity. Someone must know his background.

"When you feel better, I will show you the museum. I think you will find it of interest."

"Thank you, my lord."

The kettle was hissing. Nysander took the brown teapot down from its shelf and added some Zengati leaf and hot water.

"That's good quality," Seregil noted.

"And how do you know that?"

That won him the hint of a smile. "Fine tea smells good."

"I suppose so. Seregil, I would like to try something. A test of sorts. Would you please say the words *altra amal*?"

"Altra amal."

For just an instant every lamp in the room and the fire flared purple.

Seregil's eyes widened. "I did that?"

"You did," Nysander assured him, leaving out that the spell should have put the fire out, and not affected the lamps. Nonetheless, a genuine look of wonder had come over Seregil, and it transformed him, just as his smile had, the day Nysander met him. This young man intrigued him more and more.

"Can I try something else?" Seregil asked.

"Tea first."

He filled two earthenware cups and gave one to Seregil, who held it to his nose first and inhaled softly with eyes closed before taking his first sip. "It's excellent. Is it from the Koromba Mountains?"

"It is," Nysander told him, impressed. "Are you a connoisseur of tea?"

"No, it's one of the ones my sister always—" He broke off, and kept his attention on his cup.

So, you do have some family. Nysander wondered if this was how he'd get any information from the young 'faie, bit by tiny bit.

He let Seregil finish his tea, then took him back to the workshop. Once again Seregil looked around with keen interest, and began asking questions. A lot of questions.

"May I ask your clan?" said Nysander asked as he showed him how the astrolabe worked.

Seregil looked out through the glass dome. There was little to see at the moment. The pouring rain cloaked the city in a veil of grey. "I don't want to talk about that."

Running away again, Nysander thought. One moment he was as eager as a child, the next he was that sad, tightlipped young man again, full of secrets and pain.

"Very well. Would you like to try another spell?"

"Yes, please."

Nysander carried an unlit candle in a holder into the casting room and set it on the polished stone table at the center. "I want you to light this. Just say or think the word *'magistal'* and snap your fingers while concentrating on the wick."

With a look of eager anticipation, Seregil snapped his fingers. Instead of lighting, however, the candle flew across the room and stuck to the wall in a melted mass. "I must have thought it wrong."

"Perhaps." Nysander placed another candle in the holder. "Try again and say it aloud."

"Magistal." Seregil snapped his fingers. This time the candle softened and drooped like a wilted flower. "I guess I was right. I don't have any magic in me."

"If you didn't, then none of the spells you have cast would have had any effect at all," Nysander explained. "So you do, but there is something odd about it. Those were beginner's spells. Are you still feeling sick from the translocation?"

"A little."

"Perhaps that is the problem. And of course magic works a bit differently with your people. Well, your clothing will be dry by now. Change and I will show you the museum."

When Seregil was dressed they wended their way through the piles of documents stacked by the tower door, and out to the mezzanine that overlooked the glass-domed atrium. From here one could see the mosaic that covered the floor below; the scarlet dragon of Illior crowned with a silver crescent, flying above the harbor and walled city of Rhíminee.

"You have dragons in Skala?" asked Seregil, peering over the railing.

"Not for a very long time. But it is still one of the symbols of Illior."

"Your god that's like Aura?"

"Yes. We believe them to be one and the same."

Seregil looked doubtful as he followed Nysander down the five flights of stairs and across the atrium to the corridor leading to the museum.

It was a huge vaulted room filled with large glass cases. A whale's skeleton hung from the ceiling.

"There is a great deal to see here," Nysander said. "Let me show you a few of my favorites."

For nearly an hour Seregil moved eagerly from case to case, looking at the various artifacts as Nysander explained their use or history. There were jewels and weapons, as well as magical items that posed no threat. That sort were stored in the maze of chambers under the House.

Seregil asked more questions and Nysander was again impressed by the young man's native curiosity and quick mind. Some of the artifacts were Aurënfaie, and he seemed to take particular delight in telling Nysander what he knew of them. One case held a display of *sen'gai*, the distinctive head cloths each clan wore.

"That one's Khatme," Seregil said, pointing to a red and black weave. "And that's Golinil, and Virésse. What are they doing here?"

"Gifts to various wizards who traveled in your land, before the Edict of Separation. Do you recognize the green one?"

As he'd expected, a brief look of pain betrayed the young man. "Yes. That's Bôkthersa." He moved on to a case filled with Zengati seal rings and after a few minutes Nysander noted that he was now avoiding any case that contained Aurënfaie things.

"It would take weeks to see everything!" Seregil exclaimed at last.

"Indeed. And you are welcome to come back any time to you like to explore. We also have a very fine library."

Seregil looked like he'd just been given his heart's desire. "Thank you, my lord!"

"Please, you must call me Nysander, if we are friends now."

Seregil smiled. "Thank you, Nysander. I deeply appreciate all that you've done for me." Just then his belly gave a loud gurgle.

"Dinner time already?" Nysander laughed. The afternoon had flown by. "Dine with me, Seregil, and then I'll send you back to the palace in a carriage."

Seregil grinned. "Better than the way I got here."

Over dinner they talked of what they'd seen in the museum, and a little about Seregil's life at court."

"I understand you are no longer a junior scribe," said Nysander, chancing a conversational dead end. "May I ask why?"

Seregil gave him a rueful smile. "Emidas slapped me, and I dumped an ink pot over his head."

"Why would he slap you?"

"I hit one of the other junior scribes with a book," he replied with an almost crooked smile. "But only because he insulted me."

"I see. And what have you been doing, since?"

"I was in the household honor guard."

"Was," Nysander noted. "Did you hit someone else?"

It was as if a wall had come down between them. "No," Seregil replied, looking down at his plate.

Seregil had admitted so readily to his other infractions; what in the world had he done? Something to do with Phoria, judging by his outburst in the garden, and something that had left Seregil furious rather than shamed. Nysander again resisted the urge to touch the young man's mind. He had other, more scrupulous channels of inquiry, palace gossip being what it was.

❦

Within the week Nysander learned that Seregil's last offense had been his affair with Prince Korathan. Apparently it was Princess Phoria who'd taken exception. She had far too much hold over her brother, as far as Nysander was concerned. The prince was old enough to make his own choices, and why in the world would Phoria care, anyway? Seregil didn't speak of Korathan, and was evasive when Nysander tried to sound him out. Apparently that relationship was truly over. That was regrettable; as far as he knew, Seregil hadn't made any other friends.

He kept this knowledge to himself, and Seregil came to see him nearly every day, exploring the museum and library. The boy seemed even more thrilled by the Orëska House's elaborate bath chamber, but that wasn't all that surprising with an Aurënfaie, the cleanest of people. Much of the science of the indoor bath, including the piping of hot water under tiled floors to warm them, had been learned from them.

Seregil began to be known around the House. In fact, he seemed to be spending as much time as possible here, even when Nysander was too busy to visit with him. The keepers of the library and museum welcomed him, and Seregil began to make friends. People seemed drawn to him, whether for his good looks or sharp mind. He had winning ways, too, when he wanted to, and could be very charming and humorous. He made friends readily, apparently, and Nysander often found him talking or gaming with some of the apprentices.

Nysander watched and evaluated, and gave him little magical tests now and then, though these seldom went as planned. Seregil did have a way with animals, though and simple tricks concerning them directly came more easily to him.

As they sat over tea one day, Nysander said, "Seregil, I have a proposition for you, and I want you to consider it very carefully before you answer."

Seregil looked up in surprise. "All right. What is it?"

"You still are not happy at the palace, are you?"

"No."

"Because of what happened with Prince Korathan?"

Seregil blushed to the tips of his ears, but his tone was slightly defiant as he replied, "No, because Phoria made him stop seeing me. Korathan and I got along fine."

"But not any more?"

Seregil said nothing.

"Are you are in love with him?"

He snorted at that. "Love is for fools. I just liked him, that's all."

"I see. Thank you for being honest. I do hope you change your stance on love someday, though."

"Not likely! So, what is your proposition, exactly, and what does that have to do with it?"

"Nothing, except it is important that I know what sort of person you are before I make my offer."

"Well, you already know I'm the sort who whacks people with books and dumps ink on them. I'm no whore, though, no matter what Phoria says."

"Certainly not, dear boy! I was not thinking anything of the sort, I assure you."

"Then what is it?"

"I would like to take you on as my apprentice."

Seregil stared at him. "You—You're serious?"

"Very."

"But why? I've hardly gotten a spell right."

"You have had a few successes and I find that heartening. And you have a quick, inquiring mind, and a good memory. Those are as important in a wizard as the magic. I also enjoy your company. Given that we would work together for decades, maybe even centuries, that is important, as well. So, would you like to be my apprentice, and live here at the Orëska with me?"

"Yes!" Seregil exclaimed with no hesitation.

The wizard wasn't surprised to see tears glisten in the young man's eyes, even as he broke into the brightest smile Nysander had seen. It had no doubt been a while since anyone had told Seregil that he was wanted. Except, perhaps, for Korathan. Nysander didn't think much of how that had turned out.

"So what is your condition?" Seregil asked.

"That you tell me why you were exiled from your homeland."

In an instant Seregil's expression changed to one of pure betrayal and shame. He stood and headed for the door.

Nysander cast a lock on it from where he sat. "I will not give up on you so easily."

"Let me go," Seregil whispered, not looking at him.

"Not until you tell me."

"It doesn't make any difference! Once you know, you won't want me."

"I should like to be the judge of that."

Seregil turned to him, voice trembling with anger. "All this time—You being so nice to me. All so you ask me that?"

"Certainly not. As I said, I simply need to know what sort of person you really are."

Seregil drew himself up, glaring at him. "All right then. I killed a man. Can I go now?"

"Why did you kill him?"

"What does that matter?"

"It matters a great deal."

Seregil bit his lip. "I was somewhere I wasn't supposed to be, and he surprised me in the dark and grabbed me. I—I didn't mean to kill him. I just wanted to get away. But that doesn't change anything. So I was exiled."

"I have one last question."

"What?"

"Aside from killing that man, do you always lash out at people the way you have here?"

Seregil sighed and shook his head, hand on the door latch. "No. Can I go now?"

"That's entirely up to you, dear boy. My offer stands."

"But—after what I just told you?"

"It is up to you whether you become my apprentice or remain simply my friend who visits from a place where you are miserable. Come have some more tea while you think it over."

Seregil slowly returned to his chair by the fire, looking baffled. He took the mug and drank in silence. At last he looked up. "Why?"

"Because you were honest."

"That's it?"

"I can see how badly you want to join me here. Yet you told me the one thing that you believed would make me reject you. That shows character. Besides, wizards are sometimes called upon to kill." He sipped his tea, letting that sink in. "So?"

Seregil "Yes. I accept your offer, Nysander, with all my heart. I will try to be worthy of your regard."

Nysander leaned forward and extended his hand. "Welcome to the Third Orëska, apprentice Seregil."

The Wild

Amasa knelt behind his little son in the sun-dappled clearing, supporting his bow arm and showing him how to pull the string back. "Keep your left arm straight, Alec. Don't let your elbow bend in or the string will hit it and it will hurt."

"I can do it, Papa."

Amasa watched proudly as Alec slowly pulled the bowstring almost back to his ear. His left arm was shaking—the bow was half Alec's height, but Amasa had taken his measurements carefully while making it and Alec managed to hold his stance for a few seconds.

"That's good, child. Now ease it back."

Alec was only six, and hardly looked that, but that was old enough to start learning. Who knew when he would have to fend for himself? Skinny and sun-browned in his tunic and leggings, Alec had Amasa's thick golden hair and blue eyes, but the older he got, the more he resembled his mother. At times it broke the man's heart to look at his own son.

The clearing was loud with the sawing of summer cicadas. They were singing sooner than usual this year, thanks to the early spring. This was the danger season. They'd kept a cold campsite at night for several weeks already, drinking stream water and eating smoke-cured meat and what roots they could find.

Amasa had Alec pull the bow several more times, then handed him one of the short arrows he'd made for him. Alec nocked it to the string without being shown; he was smart and quick and had seen his father do this thousands of times. From the time he was an infant bundled on his father's back, the song of the bowstring had been his only lullaby.

"Watch me, Papa!" Alec pulled the string back again, the arrow a little wobbly, and let fly. The shaft came off badly and skittered along the ground into a patch of tall grass.

Amasa handed him another arrow. "Try again. Keep your arm up."

They practiced until Alec's arms were shaking too badly to shoot any more, then went to check their snares by the river bank. It was a lucky day; they had six muskrat pelts by afternoon, and meat to dry. Amasa nailed the skins fur side down to trees around the clearing, then scraped and buffed them clean with his knife and a smooth piece of horn. Alec followed him, rubbing each hide down with the animals' oily, cooked-down brains.

Amasa cooked some of the muskrat meat over the remains of the fire, then buried the embers and tamped the dirt down smooth.

"Time to move, child."

He helped Alec shoulder his little pack and led the way down a game trail through the thick pine forest to another clearing half a mile off. They never slept where they spent the day. With any luck, the pelts would still be there in a day or two when it was safe to go back. Amasa missed the silence of winter. The Hâzadriëlfaie man hunters didn't come looking for them then.

He and Alec were thirty miles south of Ravensfel Pass this year, but no matter how far they went, the hunters always seemed to find them. So far Amasa had managed to elude them, though he'd caught sight of them a few times from hiding places. Their leader was a slender man with grey streaks in his hair. The other riders, usually ten in all, were a mix of men and women of varying ages. They carried fine bows and long swords, too. Amasa had only his knife and bow. If it ever came to a fight at close quarters, he knew what his chances were.

He didn't recognize any of them as kin of Ireya's but it didn't matter. They hunted his son and Amasa had no illusions as to what would happen to the child if they ever found him.

Until seven years ago, Amasa had never put any stock in the legends about the Elder Folk, or the stories of travelers disappearing if they got too close to the Ravensfel. The pass was high and difficult to reach, and no doubt treacherous enough to claim the lives of those unwise enough to chance it. There was plenty of game in the forested foothills; no need to go risking his neck.

It had been a litter of white lynx that took him into the heights that fateful winter. Just one spotted pelt would bring enough gold to live on for half a year, with some left over for new gear and maybe a woman now and then. He'd seen the spoor of half a dozen cats, probably a mother and her half-grown kits. He tracked them on snowshoes for days, going higher and higher into the mountains and closer to the pass. The foothills became mountains, and the mountains turned to wooded peaks stark against the clear winter sky.

In a steep, snow-choked cut flanked on either side by thick forest, and strewn with ice-covered boulders he spotted the lynx in the distance, sunning themselves on a rocky outcropping.

It took two hours of careful stalking to get within bowshot of them and he was losing daylight. He was taking aim at the mother cat when he heard someone yell and something cold and hard struck him in the back of the head, and then another. As he turned to see who'd struck him he got a snowball square in the face that nearly broke his nose. It hurt like fire and he tasted blood on his lips. Staggering backwards, he caught one showshoe and went tumbling ass over teakettle down the steep slope he'd worked so hard to climb. The cats were long gone. So were his bow and fur hat.

Spitting blood, he untangled his snowshoes and looked for his bow. His quiver was full of snow and most of the arrows had broken fletching.

Snowballs weren't much of a weapon. Furious, he trudged back up the slope to find whoever had cost him a small fortune. As he toiled on, the thought that it might be a lost traveler leavened his anger a little, though not much. If they needed help, why annoy him first?

He found his hat and was almost back to where he'd dropped his bow when something moved behind one of the boulders up the slope near where he'd stood to shoot. Unarmed except for his knife, he crouched, watching to see if his attacker would show himself. After a moment the hint of movement came again and another snowball narrowly missed his head.

"Stop that!" he shouted angrily. "Show yourself like a man! I don't mean you any harm."

Silence followed, then his invisible adversary called out from behind the boulder, "Leave this place!"

It was a woman's voice with a strange accent. Amasa was a stubborn young man and no bitch throwing snowballs was going to drive him off. He'd worked too long following those cats and he'd find them again even if it meant going through the pass, danger be damned.

"Leave!" she shouted again.

Ignoring the order, he made a run for where she was hiding. He was within twenty feet when the woman stepped out from behind it with a bow drawn, a nasty looking steel broadhead leveled at his chest. A long knife hung at her side. Amasa put his hands up to show that he wasn't going to attack her.

She was young, and dressed in an odd fashion in a long white tunic that was split from hem to belt on either side, and worn over breeches under her white cloak. A blue-and-white striped cloth was wrapped around her head in a sort of cap with long tails. The long hair under it was dark, almost black, but her eyes were light grey. And even as he read death in those eyes, he decided that she was the most beautiful woman he'd ever seen.

Her bow arm was as steady as she held her stance. "Leave this place. Not your place, tear man!"

Tear man? What was that supposed to mean. He wasn't crying, and wasn't about to.

"Who are you?" he asked, still holding his hands out. She hadn't shot him yet, and her arm must be getting tired.

She shouted something else at him, but he didn't understand a word of it, except that she seemed angry, and perhaps a little frightened for all her bravado. Only then did it occur to him that maybe the stories of the Elder Folk were more than pipe talk. But they were supposed to have magic. This woman hadn't worked any on him yet.

Slowly, he knelt in the snow and reached inside his thick coat for a bag of rabbit jerky. He took out a piece and ate it, then tossed the bag to her. She regarded it suspiciously for a moment, then kicked it back in his direction. "Leave, tear man! My fay tast."

"I don't know what you're saying, except for the leave part," he told her. "What's your name?"

Her bow was beginning to shake a little. She released the string slowly, but kept the arrow ready on the string. "Nham?"

He touched his chest. "Amasa." Then he pointed to her. "You?"

She regarded him a moment longer. "Ireya."

It sounded like a name. "Ireya, I mean you no harm." He picked up the jerky bag, took another piece, and tossed it back to her, smiling. "Eat. It's good." Sharing food was a sign of goodwill where he came from. He hoped it meant the same to her.

Still clearly suspicious, she nonetheless set the bow aside and drew her knife. Squatting down, she fished out a piece of jerky and nibbled at it, then popped the whole piece in her mouth. "Tank you."

"So you know a little of my language. That's good." He pointed at the quickly setting sun. "Night's coming. I think we're stuck with each other 'til morning."

She glanced at the sun, then cocked her head, as if trying to puzzle out his meaning.

"Fire?" He rubbed his hands together and held them out as if over a campfire.

She hesitated again, then motioned him closer, though she kept out of arm's reach. He could see beyond the boulder now; a single line of snowshoe prints disappeared into the nearby forest. She motioned with her knife for him to go that way and to take the lead. The skin between his shoulder blades prickled as he heard her fall in behind him.

The footprints led to a camp just inside the line of trees. There was a bedroll of furs and blankets spread on packed snow beside a fire pit and a pile of scavenged firewood. Clearly she'd planned to stay the night.

She skirted the fire pit and regarded him sharply. At closer range he saw that silver earrings shaped like crescent moons hung from her earlobes. What was a rich woman doing out here by herself?

She made no objection when he dropped his pack near hers and untied his bedroll. She built a fire and produced a loaf of bread and some dried fish from a leather bag. Tearing off pieces, she offered them to him.

The bread was a little stale, but made with honey and fine flour. The fish was rubbed with some sort of herb and salt.

"Good!" he said, chewing. "Thank you, Ireya." She'd accepted his hospitable gestures, and now offered her own.

She pushed the long tails of her head cloth back over her shoulder and gave him the hint of a smile. By the Maker, but she was beautiful!

"Are you Elder Folk?" he asked, holding his hands out to the fire.

She seemed to consider the question, but did not answer. Given that she knew only a few words of his language and he knew none of hers, conversation was beyond reach for now.

The sun went down behind the peaks and the stars came out, sparkling sharply through the trees. It was going to be a cold night.

Ireya sat across the fire from him, feeding the small blaze from the woodpile, but never letting go of her knife. It didn't look like she trusted him yet, but he felt no threat from her. He tried to stay awake, but it had been a long day and sleep overtook him. When he woke at dawn the next morning, Ireya was gone, but the fire was burning and there was more bread and fish set out for him.

Amasa and Alec were stringing the muskrat pelts together a few days later when the man heard a familiar whistle in the distance. If the breeze had been blowing the other way, he probably would have missed it. The riders were no more than a mile away.

"Get your pack, Alec."

The boy was used to the terse order and asked no questions as they took up their gear and hurried down to the riverbank. Amasa picked Alec up and waded out into the current, pelts and all.

"Is the bear coming again, Papa?" Alec whispered, arms tight around his father's neck as the man stumbled downstream over the slippery stones.

"Yes, child."

Alec looked back over his father's shoulder, no doubt hoping for a sight of the bear Amasa had invented to explain these sudden departures.

Alec wished he could at least see the bad bear. Whenever it came around, his father took him to a town and left him there while he went to hunt it.

His father carried him a long way down the river, until they came to the waterfall. Alec knew this place well. There was a little cave behind the waterfall, a good place to hide from a bear. His father carried him under the torrent and into the cave, then went back for their things. Alec sat very still and quiet, so the bear wouldn't hear him.

They spent the whole day there. Alec slept for a while in the afternoon with his head on his father's leg and woke hungry and damp. They stayed there all night, too. His father went out into the woods to check for the bear a few times. That was always frightening, but Alec knew better than to say so. Papa said you should never be afraid because it made you weak and foolish.

Amasa was tracking the spotted cats higher up the snowfield the next day when he happened to look back and saw that Ireya was back. She was running in his direction and waving her arms, trying to scare off the cats again.

"Damn woman," he growled under his breath. One of the kits almost within bow shot, clearly visible in front of a rock face up the slope. He inched forward, gauging the wind. Close enough at last, he set his feet firmly in the snow and shot. The arrow struck the cat just behind the shoulder blade—a heart shot—The kit tumbled down the slope toward him until the arrow shaft caught in the snow. Shouldering his bow, Amasa began the short climb to fetch it. He could almost feel the money in his hand. Looking back again, he saw that Ireya had stopped some distance off, but was still waving her arms, frantically motioning for him to come to her.

Not without the valuable kill. Amasa was nearly to the kit when suddenly a section of glistening snow gave way beneath his feet and carried him down the slope like a wave. But waves of snow were hard as walls, and filled with rocks. It tumbled him down the slope like a man drowning in white water. Pain shot through his left forearm as he felt the sickening snap of a bone breaking. Then he and the snow were falling, falling, falling ...

Just after dawn Alec's father came back to the cave. "Come, child, we have to move on."

"Did you see the bear, Papa?" Alec asked, shivering in his damp clothes.

"Yes. He's a big one, and mean, but he's gone now. You were a good boy, keeping quiet for so long."

His father carried him and their gear out from under the falls and led Alec down the riverbed for a long time before they stopped to eat. Even though the bear was gone, his father was keeping a sharp eye out. Alec stayed quiet so he could listen. His father was a great hunter; a woman who took care of Alec sometimes told him so. Alec knew it must be a very tricky bear, not to get killed. And smart too, to always find them again.

"Are we going to the town now, Papa?" Alec whispered as he ate his cold muskrat meat.

"Yes. You'll have to stay there awhile."

"While you hunt the bear?"

"Yes, child."

"What's a bear skin worth, Papa?"

His father smiled in that tight, strange way he sometimes did. "This bear? More than you can imagine."

When they got to the town that night his father traded the pelts for silver and a few weeks of food. Then they went to the inn where they'd stayed a few nights when they came up here this spring. It was called the Coney and there was a sign shaped like a hare over the door, with painted eyes and whiskers.

The woman who ran it was kind enough, and Alec didn't mind being left here, except for the worry of having his father go away again. But Papa always came back.

Pain woke Amasa. His chest, head, and left arm ached badly, even worse than the rest of him. He felt like he'd been beaten from head to toe. He started fully awake as the memory of the avalanche came back. But he wasn't buried; he was lying wrapped in blankets and furs by a fire. It wasn't the campsite he'd shared with Ireya, but a shallow cave, the mouth of it half-filled with snow. Pushing back the furs with his good arm, he found that his left had been set and splinted with thick branches and blue-and-white rags, the same as the head cloth Ireya had worn. The rags near the middle of his forearm were stained with blood, where a sharp end of bone had broken through the skin. He had a few cracked ribs, too.

He heard the squeak of snow under boots and a moment later Ireya appeared in the mouth of the cave, carrying pair of skinned rabbits. She didn't look at him or smile as she knelt by the fire and began cutting up the meat.

"Ireya, did you bring me here?" he asked, though speaking made his chest hurt worse.

Again she didn't look at him, or answer. She was angry.

Still muddled, he lay there watching her as she cooked rabbit over the fire on a green stick. Without the head cloth, he could see how her dark brown hair shone in the firelight. Even angry, she was beautiful.

She stayed angry as they ate the rabbit and some dried apples. She had a flask of beer and grudgingly shared it with him.

She's an odd one, but must have a kind heart to dig me out of an avalanche drag me here, he thought, laying there in a nest of furs and blankets. Her furs and blankets. No doubt his were gone for good, swept away with all the rest of his gear.

"Thank you," he said at last. "Thank you for saving my life."

She seemed to understand, but it only made her madder. She spoke sharply to him in that language of hers as if she expected him to understand." When it was clear he didn't she said, "Autasa!"

Lynn Flewelling

"I don't understand, Ireya."

She snatched up the charred spit and with a few deft strokes drew the outline of a cat with spots in the dirt. "Autasa."

"The lynx kit! You're angry at me for killing it?" That was why she'd interrupted his hunt the other day. She was protecting the lynx.

"I killed your autasa. I'm sorry. I didn't know they were yours."

She just wiped out the drawing and went back to her side of the fire, but perhaps she'd understood; she now looked more sad than angry.

"Thank you for this." He held up his splinted arm, grimacing with pain.

She passed him the beer flask again, motioning for him to drink. "Turab."

He took a long swallow and felt warmth spread through him. It was strong stuff, this turab, and as good a beer as he'd ever tasted.

That night she surprised him considerably when she took off her heavy cloak and spread it over him, then got in under the bedding with him, nudging at him to give her room. Muttering something, she turned her back to him and pulled the cloak and furs up to her chin.

Amasa was in too much pain to feel any lust. Instead, he took stock of what he'd lost. Bed roll, knife, bow, extra clothing, flints, trap lines—everything that kept him alive. If it wasn't for Ireya, he'd be dead already.

She cared for him for three days, feeding him and tending his throbbing arm with snow and some sort of smelly herb he didn't recognize. She had a pouch of it and mixed up a fresh poultice each day.

On the fourth morning she brought in several loads of firewood, half a dozen skinned rabbits, and left.

She didn't come back that day, or the next, or the next and though he ate sparingly, the food was soon dwindling and the beer was gone. She'd left a cup behind and he used it over the fire to melt snow for water.

His chest and arm still ached badly, but he was well enough now to move around the cave a little. Whatever had been in those poultices had kept away fever and rot. The skin was already healing, but he knew it would take a month or more for the bones to knit, and longer before his arm was strong enough for him to draw a bow.

Just when he'd begun to give up hope of living that long, she came back, laden with a heavy pack of food and clean clothing similar to what she wore, though the tunic was shorter. There was also a knife, enough twine to make snares, and a pouch with flint, steel, and tinder shavings.

She gave him bread and slices of a hard, sharp cheese, and a sip from a flask of turab, then checked his arm, pressing here and there and sniffing the wound.

"Good," she said at last.

"Yes." The pain was down to a dull ache today.

She stayed and began teaching him words in her language. Though not enough for a real conversation, he began to get a sense of the person she was. Her folk were called Hâzadriëlfaie, and she lived on a farm somewhere beyond the peaks. Apparently it wasn't unusual for the women of her people to go off hunting.

She smiled often and sat beside him to scratch pictures in the dirt for words. He did the same with his good arm and often found himself laughing with her over his clumsy efforts. Now and then he'd catch her watching him and there was sometimes a look in her eyes that made his heart beat a little faster. He'd been with enough women to know when one fancied him. When she slept beside him again that night, Amasa was healed enough to wonder if she was doing more than keeping warm. The question was soon answered when she turned over and kissed him on the mouth, the ran her fingers down his bearded cheek and laughed softly. "Good?"

"Good." He kissed her back.

Eyes half closed, she knelt and pulled her tunic over her head. Amasa stared up at her in wonder. Her smooth skin and small round breasts looked golden in the firelight. Her nipples were like tiny wild strawberries.

It had been a long time since he'd had a woman and his breath caught in his throat as she brought his right hand up to cover her breast. They needed no common language for this. She stood to pull off her trousers, revealing slender legs and a dark triangle of hair marking her sex. She helped him out of his trouser, laughing a little at the awkwardness of it, then lay down beside him again, stroking his thigh. He ran the fingers of his good hand through her long soft hair, then down the smooth skin of her neck to cup her breast again. She sighed and kissed him, then drew a sharp breath as he gently pinched her nipple. He chuckled, then ran his hand down to her waist, her hip, her buttock. She made no complaint, but instead caressed his stiffened cock and balls, making him grow harder under her touch.

"Good!" he whispered.

She parted her thighs for him and he explored the moist lips of her cunny. She was hot and slick there already, and moaned as he took her right nipple between his lips and his fingers found that tiny, hard bud between her legs that gave women so much pleasure, gently rubbing it. A widow in Silver Bridge had shown him that spot when he was hardly more than a lad and he'd never left a woman wanting since. Ireya moaned again, rolling her hips under his hand and tightening her grip on his shaft. The musky fragrance of her cunny rose to his nostrils and he nearly came just from the smell of it. Before he could, however, Ireya threw her head back and reached her climax with a long, ragged keen, surging under his fingers. Never had he wished more for two good arms to hold her properly. Then the keen trailed off to laughter. Ireya moved his hand from between her legs and kissed him deeply as she pushed him flat on his back and straddled his hips. Holding his erection at the base, she slowly lowered herself onto it, taking him inside, into the dark tight heat of her body. Amasa groaned at the pleasure of it as she rode him. Reaching between them, he found that little bud again and played with it as she thrust herself up and down on his cock. She soon cried out again as she came and the pure joy he saw on her face pushed him over the edge into a climax of his own so intense that he could hardly catch his breath.

As they lay gasping and laughing together afterwards, Amasa held her close with his right arm and knew he felt something more than simple lust toward this woman.

❧

Ireya stayed with him for nearly a week, hunting in the daytime and making love to him by night, then disappeared as she always did, returning just before the food ran out.

"I'm going to marry you, Ireya," he whispered to her as they lay together one night. "You're going to be my wife." He wove his fingers with hers. "Do you understand? Leave with me?"

She looked down at him and their joined hands, then laughed and kissed him. "My talí."

By the time she left this time, he was well enough to go out and watch her trudge away. Her snowshoes sank deep in the glistening fresh powder and kicked up little puffs of it as she disappeared up the slope toward a small pass between two jagged peaks. There must be a town up there somewhere. Next time she went back, he meant to go with her.

But when she came back again, she wouldn't hear of it. In fact, the subject quite clearly scared her. "No, no! Kill you."

"Ireya kill me?" he asked, certain he wasn't understanding her.

She shook her head, then took up the sharp stick they used and drew a figure and pointed to herself. That was her. Then she quickly scratched out four more the same size with bows, and two larger ones. Pointing to the four, she told him, "Mine. They kill!" and poked him in the chest with her finger.

Her people would kill him. For the first time in weeks, he thought of all those stories he'd heard. Why had she befriended him, if it went against the ways of her people?

"All right, then," he sighed. "No go. You leave with me when my arm is mended."

She kissed him for that, but her eyes were sad. He didn't have the words to ask her why.

The bear came several more times that summer, and Alec's father hunted it but came back empty handed each time. Winter came, and the bear went to sleep under the snow as it always did. His father always seemed happier in the winter, even though life was harder. They set their traps and sold the skins of the muskrat, otter, mink and fisher in the towns.

But summer came again, and with it the bear.

His father took Alec back to the Coney, where the boy earned his keep sweeping and working in the garden and stables for Carsi, the innkeeper. In return he was allowed to sleep with her two young sons, who were a little older than he was, in their little airless room under the eaves, where the mice rustled through the thatch close overhead each night.

The boys, Ors and Olum, played with him when he wasn't busy. They went berrying in the forest meadows, and fishing and swimming in the river. He enjoyed it, but began to worry about his father. He'd never been gone this long before.

There was only one rider this year, the tall leader Amasa had seen before. The Hâzadriëlfaie was a cagey man, and it was clear he knew he was being stalked even as he stalked Amasa.

When Amasa did find a safe place to sleep, he dreamt of Ireya and what had happened that long ago spring. The last time she came to him in that cave had been a few weeks after the splint came off. They made love in the musky furs and then she began to cry. When he begged her to tell him why, she took his hand and placed it on her belly. The message was clear enough.

"Baby?" he asked, throat tight with emotion. A child!

"Yes," she whispered, weeping. "Kill. They will kill!"

"Kill the baby?"

She nodded.

"Then you have to come away with me. Leave with me!"

She rested her head on his broad chest and nodded. "Leave with Amasa."

But the next morning she was gone again.

He never knew if she'd changed her mind or gotten caught going back for more supplies. It didn't matter. He was strong enough now to track her, and he did, all the way up a side pass so narrow he could hardly squeeze through, to a huge valley beyond. There were scattered stone cottages and farms all the way up its length, to what looked like a town in the distance, perhaps Fay Tast, as she'd said to him that first day. Looking down from the heights, he could see riders and carts on roads, and when he crept down through the forest for a closer look, he saw they all wore the same blue-and-white head cloth—sen'gai, Ireya called it.

He had no intention of being killed before he found her, so he skulked for weeks like a wolf in the night and finally caught sight of her in the yard of an isolated farmstead not far from the narrow pass. He watched for days, but she was never out of the cottage without an escort—brothers, most likely. At night she slept in a room with iron bars on the window.

He crept to her window late one night and scratched softly at the shutter. Her face appeared there an instant later and the look she gave him was one of horror.

She reached out through the bars for his hand. "Leave!" she whispered frantically.

"No. Not without you!"

"They kill you, Amasa. They kill me! You leave!"

"I'll kill them!"

Her hand tightened on his. "No, Amasa. No kill mine!"

He could tell by her tone that she would never forgive him if he killed her kin, even to help her. "Do they know about me?"

"No," she whispered. "They wait, to see the baby."

"To see if it's Tír." He'd learned that word, the one that meant 'outsider.' "And when they do?"

"Leave," she pleaded softly, but he could see tears shining in her eyes as she turned away and closed the shutters.

But Amasa didn't. He came back night after night, but her answer was always the same. The bars were set in mortared stone. There was no getting her out that way, so he could only skulk and keep watch and bide his time.

Never once was she allowed further than the well, and not once alone. He'd come to recognize the four brothers, and the parents who lived with them. As spring gave way to summer Amasa narrowly evaded the brothers time and again and watched Ireya's belly grow round and heavy under her long tunics.

On a warm summer night the sound of a woman crying out in pain drifted up the hill to where he sheltered in the trees. Creeping down, he found too many people out in the yard to get to the window, but as the cries continued, he guessed that his child was being born, here, among his enemies. He sat in the tall grass at the edge of the forest, keeping his lonely vigil among the crickets and weeping for them both.

He was there when the sun came up, and saw Ireya slip from the silent house with a tiny bundle in her arms. Her feet were bare, her skirt bloody, her face a mask of desperation. She was making in his direction and saw him when he started down to meet her. She waved him back to the trees as she ran through the meadow and up the slope toward him. She was nearly to Amasa when her brothers came riding after her with bows.

Reaching him, Ireya thrust the swaddled infant into his arms and gasped, "Leave! Leave, talí!"

And before he could stop her, she turned and ran back the way she'd come, arms thrown wide, as if she could stop the arrows from finding him. Amasa watched in horror as she fell, then turned and bolted for the narrow pass. All he could see of the tiny babe in the swaddling was a red little face and eyes as blue as his own.

Amasa tracked his Hâzadriëlfaie hunter that summer, and his hunter tracked him. It was only a matter of time until one of them won the contest.

The Maker must have known Amasa's sorrow and taken pity on him. It was the month of Ireya's murder when, one morning just before dawn, he met his pursuer face to face. Amasa was not helpless and unarmed today, as he had been seven years ago.

The Hâzadriëlfaie man was mounted, and couldn't get his bow up in time before Amasa shot him through the lungs. Slumping over his horse's neck, the man kicked the beast into a gallop and tried to escape through the trees.

The blood trail was easily followed for a tracker like Amasa. He found a bloody bow on the ground at midmorning, and a discarded pack soon after. Just as the sun tipped down from noon, he found the man dying on the ground in a small clearing, horse nowhere in sight.

Bow drawn, Amasa came closer. The man eyed him calmly, though he must have known he was looking at his own death. "You do not understand what you do," he whispered with the same accent Ireya had had. His lips were foamed pink with lung blood, his chin crusted with it. "The child—" More blood bubbled from the corner of his mouth as he tried to speak. "Cannot be—"

"The child is," Amasa growled.

"More will come—"

Pain and hatred and old, old sorrow boiled in Amasa's heart as he spat in the man's face, pulled his head back by the hair, and slit his throat.

The rest of the day passed in a strange sort of fog, but when it cleared in the late afternoon he was covered in blood and a hide very much like a bear's was nailed to a large tree, scrapped and brain-tanned. The skinned carcass hung by its heels from another tree, gathering flies.

Let those who would come see that.

Alec was sweeping out the stable yard when his father appeared at the gate, dressed in new clothing and thinner than the boy had ever seen him. He had a string of fox and mink pelts on his belt.

"Papa!" Alec cried happily, running to him. "Did the bear get away again?"

"Not this time, child."

"You killed it! Where's the skin? How much can we sell it for?"

"It was no use for selling," his father replied. Kneeling in front of him, he held Alec by the shoulders for a moment and gazed down at him with an expression of such fondness as Alec had never seen before. Then he saw the tears in his father's eyes.

"What is it, Papa? What's wrong?" he asked, alarmed.

His father smiled. "Nothing, Alec. Not a thing. Go gather your things. We have traps to set."

By The River

Seregil leaned over the riverbank and examined the welt swelling across his left cheekbone. Angry eyes glared back up at him through the red and yellow leaves drifting past on the current: *You've failed again. Failed at court. Failed at wizardry. Failed at the assassin's craft, failed in your own birthright...Blood on your hands, but you can't even make a dishonest living.*

He dipped his left hand in the water, blotting out that accusing stare, and held it to his sore cheek. The old saying was right: hunger was a harsh master and a poor guide. It had been stupid, trying to pick the purse of a merchant in a rat hole river town full of thieves, worse even than trying to cheat those sailors at Isil two days earlier. They'd proven a good deal more clever than they'd looked, and taken everything he had—horse, sword, money, cloak, boots—before beating him senseless and dumping him on a garbage heap outside the town walls.

The merchant in Straightford had been clever, too. He must have paid some wandering drysian to charm his purse; the strings had tightened around Seregil's wrist the minute he touched silver. The man had friends on the street, too, who'd been quick to come to his aid. Seregil had barely avoided another beating, and escaped by throwing himself off a bridge into the raging river that swept through the center of the town.

He looked down at the tattered remains of the purse still clinging around his right wrist. The silken bag had torn as he fought his way to shore, and what coins it had held were lost. The charmed purse strings still bit into his flesh, too tight to pull off, and he had no knife to cut them. If he hadn't failed at all Nysander's lessons, he reflected sourly, he might have had the wit to break the charm.

Then again, if I'd had any knack for magic, I wouldn't be here, alone, barefoot and starving, in the woods at ass end of nowhere among stupid, ugly, flint-hearted Tírfaie, would I?

He sat back on his heels and gazed around, hating this foreign landscape almost more than he hated himself at the moment. The river, the road, the thick forest on every side, it wasn't so different from the lands of his father's fai'thast, yet it was.

He could go back to Rhíminee, of course; never mind all his tearful parting vows. Nysander had wept, too, when he'd left that last time, and begged him to stay, but Seregil had earned no place among wizards, only derision for his bungling.

He probably could have a place at court again, if he was willing to humble himself; he was still Queen's kin, despite the disgrace that dogged him. They'd find him some new menial office to fill. The debacles of his failed scribeship and Orëska apprenticeship would fade in time, and rumors about him and the prince. People wouldn't always laugh behind their hands when he passed.

Yes, they will.

The autumn sun was sinking fast now and he was too exhausted to go any further. And why bother? He'd been running away for months now, not going toward anything. He couldn't recall the last time he'd actually had a destination.

"Piss on that!" he growled aloud. He drank some water to calm his empty belly, then looked around for shelter. Nothing in particular presented itself, so he hobbled up the hillside to a copse and hunkered down against the sunny side of a fir tree, trying to find a comfortable angle between the roots. The sun was almost touching the distant mountain tops. The gentle breeze was going cold and finding the rents in his ragged coat and breeches.

Shivering, he pulled a foot up on his thigh and gingerly picked at a sharp stone lodged in his heel. The bottoms of his feet were filthy and covered in small scratches and cuts. As a child he wandered the forests of Bôkthersa on bare feet well callused and tough, but those days were long gone.

Better for you to have taken that boatman's offer in Isil, the mocking voice in his head went on. *At least you'd be under a roof. He'd probably even have stood you a tavern meal after, if you'd played him right ...*

A wave of despair washed over him. Not for the first time, he wondered why he hadn't done as the others had years ago: filled his pockets with ballast stones and thrown himself overboard that first day of exile, when his homeland slipped away under the horizon behind the ship.

The glint of sun on water winked at him through the trees below. There was nothing to stop him from doing it now, except that he was too cold, too tired, and too miserable to muster the energy it would take to walk back down to the bank and throw himself in.

He must have nodded off. Otherwise a Tírfaie would never have gotten as close as this one had. As it was, he just had time to throw himself into a nearby clump of caneberry bushes before the man stepped from the trees less than twenty feet from where he'd been sitting. Scratched and shaken, Seregil peered out through the thorny stalks, watching the intruder stroll up the hill.

The last glow of sunset was at the man's back, casting long shadows in front of him. All Seregil could make out at first was a tall, broad-shouldered figure, with a long scabbard swinging heavily against its left hip.

The man halted near the tree, then looked around. "Hullo?" A young, deep voice, colored by an accent Seregil couldn't place. "Don't be scared, girl. I won't hurt you."

Girl? Seregil allowed himself a sour smile. Stupid, blind fool of a Tírfaie, just like all the others. By the Light, he was sick of the whole lot.

All the same, this one had gotten dangerously close, and Seregil couldn't move now without being heard. Looking quickly around, he found a fist-sized rock in reach and gripped it.

The fellow turned slightly and the light struck his face. He was man-grown but still young by Tír reckoning. His face was strongly boned, and freckled as a trout's sides. Coarse auburn hair hung in an unkempt mass over his shoulders. A sparse, coppery moustache drooped over the corners of his mouth and his cheeks and chin were thatched with stubble. His battered corselet and worn boots marked him as a wanderer of some sort, at best a caravan guard; at worst, a bandit.

Harsh experience had taught Seregil something of reading faces; this man was not stupid, not at all. All the time he was gazing about, he seemed to have an ear cocked in Seregil's direction. *He knows I'm here.* Seregil gripped the rock, bracing for an attack. If he could surprise the man, stun him with a well-placed blow, then he could escape, perhaps even with the sword and that bundle the man had over his shoulder. He didn't look the sort to travel without food or flints.

But the man just stood there a moment longer, then shrugged. "Suit yourself, girl." With that, he dropped his bundle and set about gathering sticks and tinder for a fire.

Sprawled on the damp ground, Seregil watched with growing suspicion as the fellow struck a spark with his knife and a flint and kindled a good blaze under the tree. When it was burning well, he rummaged in his bundle and brought out a small iron pot and a few cloth-wrapped parcels. Leaving his supplies by the fire, he headed down to the river with the pot.

It was tempting to make a dash for the supplies, but it was obviously a ruse to draw him out. Seregil stayed where he was, and presently the man came back with his pot and some green ash sticks he'd cut at the riverbank. He rigged up a fire hook with some of them and set the pot of water over the flames. Then he sharpened another stick with his knife, unwrapped the parcels, and fixed a large chunk of yellow cheese and some sausages on the stick to toast.

Soon a mouth-watering aroma spread over the little clearing. Seregil's stomach, empty these past two days except for river water and what little he could forage, let out a long growl.

As if he'd heard, the man called out, "More than enough for two here, girl. From the glimpse I got of you, I'd say you could use something solid under your ribs. And a blanket, too. I won't ask to share it with you. I swear by the Flame and the Four."

Seregil remained where he was, hating the man even more.

"Come now, I know you're there. That raspberry patch won't make much of a bower for you when the dew falls." After a long moment, the fellow let out an exasperated sigh. "No? Well, I won't force you out, but I don't fancy sleeping with you lurking there like that, so we're both in for a weary night."

Seregil lay still, mouth watering, as the dew settled through his scant clothing, chilling him from the back as the damp ground chilled him from the front. The sausages sizzled on their stick, redolent of rosemary, mutton, and garlic. He hadn't smelled anything so good since the market stalls at Cirna. By the Light, how long ago? Two years? Three? The aroma reminded him suddenly of Nysander, too. His old master had always had good sausage like that at breakfast, and toasted cheese. And soft white bread with honey and jam.

He ached with hunger now, and something else, too. Something that made his throat tighten and his eyes sting.

It was almost certainly a trick, he thought, blinking away the smoke that had blurred his vision for a moment. He flexed the fingers that had gone stiff around the rock. This was no bandit. This man knew how to wait, how to bait his prey. That was warning enough.

All the same, he could just as easily have come after him. The man knew where he was, and assumed he was dealing with a defenseless girl. Why all the calling and courting?

Seregil wrestled with his doubts a little longer, but the smell of hot food weighted the argument against caution. At last he called out, "What do you want with me?"

His voice came out hoarse as a rook's; he hadn't spoken to anyone in days.

"Nothing," the man replied, lifting the meat and cheese from the fire and examining them closely. "This is about ready."

Still not looking in Seregil's direction, he reached into his bundle again and threw something into the steaming pot. A moment later Seregil smelled the sharp, rich tang of tea. Real tea from Zengat by the smell, not the stinking mess of boiled leaves and roots they brewed up here in the wilderness.

"I've an extra mug here somewhere, girl. You're welcome to it."

That decided it. Either this was a civilized fellow, or he knew enough to steal from such. Seregil stood up slowly, braced to run if the man proved treacherous after all. "I'm not a girl," he croaked.

The man looked over at him and his moustache twitched in what might have been a grin. "So you're not. My apologies, lad. You ran off so fast I didn't have time to make a proper study of you. You won't be needing that, though you're welcome to hang onto it if it makes you feel any safer."

Seregil glanced down and saw that he was still clutching the rock. No doubt he looked ridiculous to the big swordsman, but he kept it anyway.

"Come on if you're hungry," the man urged. "I'm not getting up to serve you."

Seregil pulled himself free of the thorny canes and limped to the fire, giving the stranger a wide berth and keeping the fire between them. The man stayed where he was, but leaned over to hand Seregil the toasting stick.

He took it, and watched warily as the man found a cup and tossed it over to him. He caught it easily and set it down beside him.

"Welcome. My name's Micum," his host said, resting his large hands on his knees where Seregil could see them, clearly a calculated move to show he meant no harm. Seregil ignored the expectant pause that followed. He gave his name to no Tír.

"I don't have a knife," he said at last. In fact, it was all he could do not to gnaw the meat and cheese straight off the toasting stick, but that would have been common, and poor thanks for the hospitality offered.

The stranger drew the knife from his belt and held it out, handle foremost.

Seregil tensed again. If he reached for it, distracted with food and one hand busy with the stick, it would be a simple matter for the other man to grab for his wrist.

He'd hardly finished the thought when Micum placed the knife on the ground between them and sat back. "You're a cautious one, aren't you? Though from the looks of you, maybe you have good cause to be."

It was nearly dark now, but the firelight shone full on his face and for the first time Seregil was able to look him in the eye at close range. Light eyes, he had, bright at the moment with friendly amusement. Seregil snatched up the knife and cut the purse string from his wrist, then carved himself a portion.

"You'll want this, too." Micum tossed a chunk of stale brown bread neatly over the fire and into Seregil's lap.

Seregil took a second look at him, guessing that this move had been a sign, too. This man knew how to fight and wanted him to know it; the scabbard hanging overhead was scarred with use and he had a few scars on the backs of his hands. He was big, nearly a head taller than Seregil, and well muscled, but he moved with a natural, fluid grace. Fine swordsman that Seregil was when he had a sword, he already suspected that this Micum fellow was someone

he'd rather fight beside than against. He'd made no move to harm Seregil yet, either, but the evening was still young.

"I'll have the knife back, if you're done with it," Micum said, watching the stranger closely without making a show of it. He was beginning to regret his kindly impulse.

Not only was this no lost girl, as he'd first supposed when he'd glimpsing the huddled figure from the road; this ragged, wild-haired fellow wasn't as young as he'd first guessed, either. No, he was 'faie—true pure Aurënfaie, too, judging by his build, his high-tone manner of speech, and the southern cut of his rags. What a 'faie was doing here on the banks of the Keela River, only Illior knew. No gear. No horse. No food. Thin and dirty as a young tom in spring, and just as battered. Someone had given him a proper drubbing recently, and perhaps he'd deserved it. There was a toughness about him that balanced that fine, pretty face, and a hard glint in those cold grey eyes that Micum didn't like one bit; it was the look of a kicked dog that was ready to bite. He hadn't given his name like an honest man, either.

And, Micum noted with no particular alarm, he still had the knife. He held out his hand for it, and the bottom nearly dropped out of his belly as the stranger handily flipped it up in the air, caught it by the blade, and shied it at him.

Either the man's aim was very good or a little bad, for the blade thudded to earth a few inches from Micum's left knee, the quivering blade sunk a good three inches in the ground. Judging by the fellow's smirk, this was a message to him, and Micum added arrogance to the rapidly growing list of reasons why he didn't like this nameless stray.

All the same, he had given the knife back. Micum pulled it free and wiped the blade clean on his trouser leg before cutting his own portion. "You're an Aurënfaie, aren't you?" he asked, to see if he could take him down a peg. "Up from Skala, I'd say, by your accent and those rags. You're a long way from home."

This earned him a startled look. His guest didn't look quite so smug now. "I am. I don't recognize your accent."

"I don't suppose you would," Micum replied, fighting back a grin. "I'm from a little town in the free holdings beyond the Folcwine. Cavish, it's called."

"Never heard of it. Is that in Mycena?"

"North and east beyond it. I've been working the Gold Road as a guard for the caravaneers. I liked what I've heard of the southern lands, and I liked the men I worked for. The caravaneers were full of tales of Skala and her fine cities, so when we got to Nanta, I decided to keep on going and have a look for myself."

"Just like that?"

"Just like that."

Suddenly the stranger surprised him again, this time with a smile . "So you're a long way from home, too."

Micum blinked. It was as if a completely different person was looking at him from under all the dirt and tangled hair. The hard, guarded look had slipped like a mask, showing Micum someone almost as young as he'd first supposed. He was shivering, too, Micum saw; the hand holding the bread was shaking so badly that the cheese was sliding off.

Micum untied his cloak and gave it to him, still careful not to move too suddenly and startle him. "You'd best wrap up."

"Thank you." The stranger accepted it with a rather chagrinned look.

Balancing his supper on one knee, he bundled himself up to the chin as if it was winter, rather than a warm autumn night. With his rags covered, he had a more refined look about him, even with the dirty face. Micum hadn't had a lot of contact with folk of quality, but he knew one when he met one and this boy was gentle born, whatever his circumstances might be now. He chewed his food slowly, rather than wolfing it, then dipped his cup in the pot and held it to his nose, eyes half closed as he inhaled the fragrant steam.

"It's been a long while since I've had this," he murmured.

"Got a taste for it from those Skalans," Micum told him, studying his guest with growing interest. "I'd rather have good ale, myself, but this carries easier and refreshes the spirits."

The stranger saluted him with the cup, poured out a few drops on the ground for whatever gods he owned, and then sipped delicately at the brew. Micum filled his own cup and they sat in silence for awhile as the stars came out overhead.

As the tea spread its comforting warmth through him, Seregil let out a contented sigh. Micum's cloak was warm and smelled good. The man had given freely of his food and offered him no violence. As the comfortable silence stretched out between them, he allowed himself a second look at his companion. Micum wasn't handsome, certainly, but he had a good smile and a steady, easy manner that put Seregil at his ease. It was tempting, so very tempting, to like him.

More fool, you, the inner voice taunted.

Ignoring it, he arched a wry eyebrow at Micum. "So you don't mean to rob or rape me, after all?"

"Is that what you thought?" Micum asked, insulted. "And rob you of what, pray tell?"

"I'm sorry," Seregil said hastily. "I ask your pardon. I haven't had much cause to trust anyone for a long while. But tell me, why did you come up here after me?"

The man looked as if he'd asked why the sky was blue. "I saw you from the road. You looked like someone who needed help."

"A girl who needed help," Seregil reminded him.

Micum shrugged. "It makes no difference."

Seregil looked into that earnest face and felt his resolve slipping again. *Stop it! He's a Tír. Nothing but a Tír ...*

"You don't believe me?" Micum bristled again.

"Oh, I do," Seregil assured him, looking down into the fire to avoid that earnest gaze. "I do."

"Then I don't suppose I might know who I'm talking to?"

Fool! the voice shrieked as Seregil leaned over and offered his hand to the man. "Forgive my rudeness. I'm..." He faltered as Micum's big, rough hand closed around his. The man's grip was warm, firm, reassuring, and came in the company of a ready smile. Seregil had to swallow hard before he could finish. "I'm Rolan. Rolan Silverleaf."

The Bond

Watermead

Something brushed Alec's hand and he opened one eye, expecting to see Illia or one of the dogs.

Nysander was standing beside the bed.

"Go after him," Nysander whispered, his voice faint as if it came from a great distance.

Alec lurched up, his heart pounding. Nysander had disappeared, if he'd ever been there at all.

Worse yet, Seregil was gone. Alec slid his hand over the sheets where Seregil had slept. They were cold.

Whether dream or vision, the urgency of Nysander's warning grew stronger by the second.

Scrambling out of bed, Alec hauled on breeches and a shirt and headed for the door. His bare foot struck something as he crossed the threshold. It was a thick roll of parchments bound with plain string.

Untying it, he quickly scanned the familiar flowing script covering the first page.

"Alec talí, remember me kindly and try—"

"Damn!" Pages scattered in all directions as Alec ran for the stables.

Too much to hope that Seregil had gone on foot; Cynril was missing from her stall. Mounted bareback on Patch, Alec searched for and quickly found Cynril's tracks, the distinctive print of the slightly splayed right hind hoof plain in the dust of the road outside the courtyard gate.

Kicking Patch into a gallop, he rode down the hill and across the bridge, reining in where the two roads met to see which way Seregil had gone.

But there was no sign of Cynril here. Cursing softly to himself, Alec dismounted for a closer search, then walked back onto the bridge and scanned the hillside, looking for telltale lines across the dewy meadow. Nothing there either, or on the hill trail. He was about to ride back for Micum when a patch of freshly turned gravel on the stream bank above the bridge caught his eye.

You went up the streambed, you sneaky bastard! Alec thought with grudging admiration. The bridge was too low to ride under and there were no other signs downstream. Upstream lay Beka's otter pond, and the ill-fated pass that Alec had crossed to Warnik's valley.

And beyond that, the whole damn world.

Mounting again, Alec rode up the trail. The streambed grew steeper and he soon found where Seregil had been forced to come up onto the trail. Judging by the tracks, he'd traveled quickly from here.

Heedless of the branches that whipped at his face and shoulders, Alec kicked Patch into a gallop again. When the clearing around the pond came into view ahead, he was both relieved and surprised to see Seregil there, sitting motionless in the saddle as if admiring the morning.

Alec's first reaction to Seregil's letter had been only the desperate desire to find him. He realized now that there had also been a generous leaven of anger mixed in. When Seregil raised his head now, looking back at him with an expression of startled wariness, the anger took over. It was the look you'd give an enemy.

Or a stranger.

"Wait—" Seregil called, but Alec ignored him. Digging his heels into Patch's sides, he charged Seregil, bearing down on him before he could turn his own horse out of the way. The animals collided and Cynril reared, throwing Seregil off into the water. Alec leapt down and waded in after him. Grabbing Seregil by the front of his tunic, he hauled him to his knees and shook the crumpled note in his face.

"What's this supposed to be?" he yelled. "'All I have in Rhíminee is yours now'? What is this?"

Seregil struggled to his feet and pulled free, not meeting Alec's eye. "After everything that's happened—" He paused, took a deep breath. "After all that, I decided it would be better for everyone if I just went away."

"You decided. *You* decided?" Furious, Alec grabbed Seregil with both hands and shook him. The wrinkled parchment drifted across the pool, hung a moment against a stone, and spun away unnoticed down the stream. "I followed you over half the earth to Rhíminee for no other reason than you asked me to! I saved your damn life twice before we even got there and how many times since? I stood with you against Mardus and all the rest. But now, after moping around all summer, you decide you're better off without me?"

Color flared in Seregil's gaunt face. "I never meant for you to take it that way. Bilairy's Balls, Alec, you saw what happened at the Cockerel. That was my fault. Mine! And it was only thanks to Ashnazai's twisted vanity that you didn't end up dead with them. Micum's crippled for life, in case you didn't notice, lucky to be alive. Do you have any idea how many times I've almost gotten him killed before? And Nysander—Let's not forget what I did for him!"

"Nysander sent me!"

Seregil went ashen. "What?"

"Nysander sent me after you," Alec told him. "I don't know if it was a dream or a ghost or what, but he woke me and told me to go after you. Illior's Hands, Seregil, when are you going to forgive yourself for just doing what he asked you to?"

He paused as another thought dawned on him. "When are you going to forgive Nysander?"

Seregil glared at him wordlessly, then pushed Alec's hands away. Sloshing up to the bank, he sank down on a log overlooking the pond. Alec followed, settling on a rock beside him.

Seregil hung his head and let out an unsteady breath. After a moment he said, "He knew. He should have told me."

"You would have tried to stop him."

"Damn right I would have!" Seregil flared, clenching his fists on his knees. Angry tears spilled down his cheeks, the first Alec had ever seen him shed.

"If you'd done that, we'd have failed," Alec said, moving to sit beside him on the log. "Everything Nysander worked for would've been lost. The Helm would have taken him over and he'd have ended up as their Vatharna."

For an instant Alec thought he felt the wizard's touch against his hand again. "I think he must be grateful to you."

Seregil covered his face, giving way at last to silent sobs. Alec wrapped an arm around him, holding him tightly. "You were the only one who loved him enough not to hesitate when the time came. He knew that. In the end you saved him the only way you could. Why can't you let yourself see that?"

"All these weeks—" Seregil shrugged helplessly. "You're right, right about everything. But why can't I feel it? I can't feel anything anymore! I'm floundering around in a black fog. I look at the rest of you, see you healing, going on. I want to, but I can't!"

"Just like I couldn't make myself jump that time at Kassarie's keep?"

Seregil let out a small, choked laugh. "I guess so."

"So let me help you, the way you helped me then," Alec persisted.

Seregil wiped his nose on his sodden sleeve. "As I recall, I threw you off the roof into a gorge."

"Fine, if that's what it takes to show you that I'm not about to let you slink away like some old dog going off to die."

The guilty look that crossed his friend's face told Alec his worst fears had been correct. "I'm not letting you go," he said again, gripping Seregil's sleeve for emphasis.

Seregil shook his head miserably. "I can't stay here."

"All right, but you're not leaving me."

"I thought you'd be happy at Watermead."

"I love everyone there like my own family, but not—" Alec broke off, feeling his face go warm.

"But not what?" Seregil turned and brushed a clump of damp hair back from Alec's face, studying his expression.

Alec forced himself to meet Seregil's questioning gaze squarely. "Not as much as I love you."

Seregil looked at him for a moment, grey eyes still sad. "I love you, too. More than I've loved anyone for a long time. But you're so young and—" He spread his hands and sighed. "It just didn't seem right."

"I'm not that young," Alec countered wryly, thinking of all they'd been through together. "But I am half faie, so I've got a lot of years ahead of me. Besides, I've only just begun to understand Aurënfaie, I still don't know one style of snail fork from another, and I can't jigger a Triple Crow lock. Who else is going to teach me all that?"

Seregil looked out over the pond again. "Father, brother, friend, and lover."

"What?" A coldness passed over Alec's heart; Mardus had spoken almost those same words when asking about his relationship to Seregil.

"Something else the Oracle of Illior said that night I asked about you," Seregil answered, watching an otter slip into the water. "I kept thinking I had it all sorted out and settled, but I don't. I've been the first three to you and swore that was enough, but if you stay on with me—"

"I know." Catching Seregil off guard, Alec leaned forward and pressed his lips to Seregil's with the same mix of awkwardness and determination he'd felt the first time. But when he felt Seregil's arms slip around him in a welcoming embrace, the confusion that had haunted him through the winter cleared like fog before a changing wind.

Take what the gods send, Seregil had told him more than once.

He would, and thankfully.

Seregil drew back a little, and there was something like wonder in his grey eyes as he touched Alec's cheek. "Anything we do, tali, we do with honor. Before all else, I'm your friend and always will be, even if you take a hundred wives or lovers later on."

Alec started to protest but Seregil smiled and pressed a finger across his lips. "As long as I have a place in your heart, I'm satisfied."

"You always have to have the last word, don't you?" Alec growled, then kissed him again. The feel of Seregil's lean body pressing against his own suddenly felt as natural and easy as one stream flowing into another. His last remaining worry was that he had very little idea about how to proceed from here.

It was almost like an ordinary day at Watermead after that, the same as any other visit. Only it wasn't. Even after their admission by the otter pool, Alec could sense the lingering sadness that still clung to Seregil. It was too much to hope, he supposed, that all that had happened this morning was enough to heal the wounds his friend carried. When Seregil noticed Alec watching him, he always brightened and smiled, but when he thought no one was looking the light faded a little. So Alec kept an eye on him and kept his own council. He caught Seregil watching him, too, looking a little worried. He wondered if he was beginning to regret his words that morning.

Anything we do, tali, we do with honor.

Things had changed between them, at the otter pool.

They might have changed in a worse direction if Alec hadn't gotten there in time. The thought of Seregil trying to leave him behind still hurt.

Seregil seemed determined to keep them busy around the farm, carrying in water and firewood for Kari, helping Micum tend a horse with a sore on its

leg, and driving a wagon to a field where the hired men were haying. As they rode back with a load, Alec seized the opportunity.

"Were you going off to die this morning?"

Seregil was quiet for a moment, staring down the track ahead of them, reins slack in his hands. "I don't know," he said at last. "Maybe. I'm sorry I scared you."

"Don't do it again."

"I won't." Seregil turned to him, his expression solemn. "You have my word, Alec. *Rei phöril*—"

Alec clasped his shoulder. "Don't. I don't need any oaths from you. You said you'd never lie to me, and I believe you."

"Thank you." Seregil smiled—a real smile—and kissed him.

Alec's breath caught in his throat; it was the first time that Seregil had initiated a kiss between them. He had questions of a different nature, too, but he couldn't seem to find the words, out here in daylight.

Anything we do—

He couldn't help thinking of the night he'd found Seregil lounging in that green light brothel in the Street of Lights and the first stirring of attraction he'd felt then—for now Alec understood what that had been. The highly detailed murals on the walls there had left him with no doubt as to the sort of pleasures men found with each other. Some of it wasn't all that different from what he'd done with Ylinestra and Myrhichia, only—who did what to who when it was both men? Despite occasional good natured teasing, Seregil had never touched directly on the subject in any detail, and Alec was left with nothing but a vague mix of anticipation and unease, and concern for Seregil. This morning he'd been ready to go off and die. Maybe Alec was expecting too much?

By supper time he was willing the sun to sink faster, so that they could finally be alone to sort things out. As he sat with Seregil and the Cavishes by the hearth afterwards, holding little Gherin for Kari so she could knit, he began to feel increasingly nervous and awkward. Seregil was yawning, obviously worn out.

Alec grew more and more quiet, the closer they got to the end of the evening, and Seregil was aware of the way Alec's gaze fixed on him when he thought Seregil wasn't looking. It was more than ale or the hearth fire that kept that persistent pink flush in his friend's smooth cheeks. It deepened to an outright blush when old Arna asked Alec if he felt all right.

The certainty Seregil had felt that morning was slipping. *It's too soon. I have no right.*

But his traitor memory played the words of the Oracle over and over again: *Father, brother, friend, and lover.* Alec's poignantly innocent kisses on that Plenimaran beach and today left him with no doubt that they were no longer merely friends, much less master and apprentice. They'd forged a bond built on shared trust and hardship. They owed each other their lives. Seregil wasn't exactly sure when he'd fallen in love with Alec; it had taken him this long to admit it.

Friend. Lover?

Seregil remembered his first hesitant embraces with Ilar, the mix of fear and thrill and muddled desire. As much as he'd later come to hate the lying son of a bitch, he had to admit that Ilar had been the perfect first lover: gentle, patient, and asking for so little. There hadn't been much opportunity for privacy at that summer encampment. They'd never even been naked with each other. All the same, Seregil had loved him and lived for his caresses until Ilar broke his heart and changed his life forever.

It hadn't really prepared him for his first night in Prince Korathan's bed, less than a year later. It wasn't love that put him there, but desperate loneliness. The young prince had been kind, too, but less patient and far less restrained than Ilar. Only then did Seregil realize that his love making with Ilar had been little more than foreplay. Korathan expected—and got—a lot more than that from Seregil, right from the start. Seregil had hardly been able to get out of bed the first few mornings. Fortunately Korathan had been as careful to give pleasure as he was determined to receive it. Seregil hadn't loved him, but was grateful for the sense of peace he'd found for a little while in the young man's strong arms. And that had ended abruptly and painfully, too, when Phoria caught them together one night.

He meant to do better than that by Alec.

Seregil wanted more than that.

He hardly realized how far his mind had strayed until Kari set her knitting aside and took Gherin from Alec's arms. "Seregil, Alec's about to go to sleep in his chair after the long day you gave him. Go to bed, both of you."

She smiled as she said it, but it felt like she'd read his thoughts. Was it his guilty imagination, or did her look hold a warning?

Micum stood and stretched, then scooped up Luthas, who'd been playing with a horn spoon at his feet. "Good night! And remember; I want a sword match with you tomorrow, Alec!"

"I'll be ready. I still have a few patches of skin that aren't bruised."

Finally alone, Seregil and Alec sat staring into the fire in silence. Knowing they'd probably spend the rest of the night like that if he didn't do something, Seregil stood and held out a hand. Pulling Alec to his feet, Seregil took him in a loose embrace.

Alec hugged him back, but there was hesitation in his voice as he said, "You need some sleep."

"It's all right."

Alec rested his head on Seregil's shoulder for a moment, then took his hand and led him into the bed chamber they'd shared so chastely.

Arna had banked the guest room hearth. Warmth lingered in the air, and with it the scent of pine kindling and the mingled perfume of carved cedar wood and sweet strewing herbs. The night wind sighed softly in the chimney, making the tinkling embers glow red under a thin pall of ash. Mice stirred restlessly in the thatch over the rafters and a lonely cricket chirped from some shadowed corner.

Alec came to a halt beside the bed, then took him by the shoulders far more gently than he had at the pond and kissed Seregil again in that firm, earnest way of his. Unskilled as he was, there was a naked honesty to it that warmed even the coldest, most shadowed reaches of Seregil's battered heart.

"Talí." It was the only thing Seregil could think of that encompassed everything he felt right now.

Alec smiled. "You called me that by accident the first time, remember?"

"Unthinking, perhaps, but no accident."

Alec's cheeks went crimson as he declared softly, "You're my talí, too."

Something was going to happen tonight, Alec knew; something that would probably change the way they looked at each other forever. Seregil was his friend. Alec didn't want that to change, and yet he did.

They stood there for a moment in each other's arms. "What now?"

Seregil's chuckle sent a tickling vibration through his chest. "There's nothing to be scared of."

"I'm not scared!" It didn't sound very convincing, though, and he felt his face go red.

"You're my friend, Alec, and my talí. You and no other. If you don't want this, it doesn't change anything for me."

Alec tightened his arms around Seregil's waist. He could feel Seregil's heart beating hard against his own. Warm fingers caressed the back of his neck. Warm lips kissed his forehead. Seregil said nothing but Alec knew he was waiting for an answer.

He kissed Seregil and murmured, "What do we do now?"

"Bed." Seregil released him, then shucked off his clothes. He was thinner than usual, thanks to his summer of mourning, but still as beautiful in Alec's eyes as ever. Then he noticed with a pang of embarrassment that Seregil's cock wasn't stiff in that patch of dark hair. Neither was his, for that matter. "Something's wrong."

Seregil smile. "No, it's not."

Blushing furiously, Alec looked away and began to undress, but when he was down to his long shirt Seregil caught his hand and stopped him. "Lie down."

Alec's heart beat against his ribs as he pulled back the quilts and slipped between the clean, sun freshened sheets. It beat a little harder as Seregil climbed in beside him.

Lifting Alec's right arm out of the way, Seregil slid under it to settle close beside him with his head on Alec's chest and his arm snug around Alec's waist. Then he yawned and Alec felt the tension leave his friend—his talí's—body. Something of the feeling of their morning embrace came back to him; this felt easy and right. Heat settled in Alec's belly as he stroked Seregil's silky brown hair and watched the shifting shadows above the rafters, enjoying the soft rhythm of Seregil's breath against his chest through the thin material of his shirt. He'd slept beside Seregil many times, but never like this.

After a few minutes Seregil looked up at him. "I still see questions in your eyes."

Alec hesitated, screwing up his courage to finally voice his main concern. "Remember when I found you at that green lantern brothel?"

Seregil grinned. "It was quite the memorable moment."

"Well—" This was as difficult as trying to make himself jump from the tower of Kassarie's keep! But this time he managed it without being thrown. "It's just—I've been thinking of those murals."

Seregil raised an amused eyebrow. "You want a tavern board to choose from?"

"No! I just—I'm not so sure I want to do some of those things. A lot of those things!"

"Forget all that." Seregil smoothed a stray strand of blond hair away from Alec's cheek. "I think I know what you'll like tonight. And you can always say so when you don't."

Alec paused, then shifted away just enough to pull off his shirt without elbowing Seregil in the face. Then he kicked back the covers.

Seregil's eyes widened, no doubt surprised at this breach of Alec's usual modesty. Then he leaned forward and kissed Alec, sliding the tip of his tongue lightly across Alec's closed lips. Strange thing to do, but it felt surprisingly good, so Alec did it back. This won him a hum of approval. He could feel the long hardness of Seregil's shaft against his hip now, and his own against his belly.

Pulling back a little, he gasped, "Show me."

And Seregil, ever the willing teacher, did so, slowly at first, with fingers, lips, and tongue, touching him in ways that made Alec gasp and shiver. Seregil showed him sensitive places he didn't even know he had: the side of his neck, the crook of an elbow, an ankle, behind his balls. Drowning in sensation, he lay there, letting Seregil do what he wanted; this was like nothing he'd ever felt, not even with Myrhichia. His cock ached but Seregil didn't touch it, even when Alec began to move under his hands, trying to coax him there.

Seregil chuckled softly, then stretched out beside him and kissed Alec's right knee. Then just above it, and a bit higher, and then a little higher, slowly working his way to the edge of the small island of dark blond curls at the base of his shaft. Alec's breath quickened as Seregil swirled his tongue across the sensitive skin between there and his hipbone. Myrhichia had taken him in her mouth and pleasured him with her tongue. That had been exciting and pleasurable, but it was all the more so when Seregil did the same, and with skills rivaling those of the courtesan. Stroking Seregil's hair with shaking fingers, he was half aware of his own whispered, incoherent pleas for release. But Seregil stopped too soon. Far too soon.

"Not yet, talí," Seregil said, tracing the length of Alec's shaft with his tongue one last time from root to foreskin. He guided Alec up to sit with his back to Seregil's chest and began kissing and nipping at the back of his neck and across his shoulders, all the while caressing his chest and belly, just a few tantalizing inches from where Alec most wanted to be touched again.

Seregil murmured something in Aurënfaie against his skin.

"What?"

"My heart is yours forever."

"So is mine—" Alec gasped as a thumb skimmed his left nipple. "Yours, I mean."

Seregil laughed softly, a deep, rich throaty laugh, then licked Alec's ear and teased the stiffened nipple again between two fingers.

Alec felt a little faint. Ylinestra had been domineering and had cheated with magic; Myrhichia had been sweet and kind. For the first time now, Alec experienced the confluence of love and sex and it was better than any magic.

Too good, in fact. When Seregil took Alec's cock in his hand and stroked it as he nipped at that place where Alec's neck met his shoulder, it was too much. Alec arched in his arms, vision gone white in a long agony of pleasure, and came all over his chest, belly, and Seregil's hand. Mortified beyond words, he weakly tried to struggle free, but Seregil held him tight.

"It's all right, talí. I take it as a compliment," Seregil murmured against his cheek, then licked one glistening finger, like it was coated with honey.

Alec felt a fresh spike of desire . He found his discarded shirt and wiped away the mess. Then, twisting around in the circle of his lover's arms, he cradled Seregil's balls in one hand and ran his fingers up the length of his smooth, hard length with the other, amazed at the weight of another man's cock in his hand. "Show me more."

Seregil had never seen anyone look so innocent and so wanton at the same time, but somehow Alec managed it. That, and Alec's amazingly sure touch, nearly undid him. Pulling Alec down with him, Seregil whispered, "Touch me the way I touched you."

Alec had always been an apt pupil, and this was no exception. Seregil swallowed something dangerously close to a giggle as he thought, *if only he was this quick learning sword play!*

Kneeling on the bed beside him, Alec ran his hands over Seregil's chest and sides. The tips of the fingers on his right hand were slightly rough from pulling a bowstring. Seregil shivered deliciously as those hands roamed further afield, over his shoulders, down the insides of his thighs. He cursed softly in delight as Alec traced the arch of his foot with his tongue. Then he kissed him from throat to navel, soft blond hair raising gooseflesh as it brushed Seregil's skin, but stopped just short of Seregil's cock.

Hesitant, or revenge? Seregil wondered with amusement. It soon proved to be neither as Alec licked the tip and closed his hand around the shaft, stroking him in a perfect rhythm.

All too quickly the ecstasy shook through Seregil in waves, pulling a strangled snarl of pleasure from deep in his chest as he came hard and long in Alec's hand. Helplessly undone, he laid there, chest heaving, as Alec lay down beside him.

He found Alec's hand and gripped it. "Thank you."

Alec grinned, looking rather proud of himself.

Happy. Seregil felt so damn happy. The despair and self pity of the night before seemed like a bad dream. They lay there together for a while, listening to the night breeze and the beating of each other's hearts. When his head finally stopped spinning, Seregil rolled on top of Alec and kissed his way down the side of his lover's neck. "Your turn."

✤

The night candle burned down to the socket and guttered out before they fell, sated, against the bolsters, sweat cooling on their skin. Alec yawned widely, eyelids already heavy. "Sorry."

Seregil gave him a fond smile. "Nothing to apologize for, talí." Turning on his side, he pulled Alec back against his chest and kissed him on the back of the head. "Everything was perfect. Go to sleep."

Alec was, almost before Seregil had finished speaking. But Seregil lay awake a little longer, thinking of all the times they'd nearly lost each other. But Alec's scent and heat soothed away the dark thoughts.

"Forever, talí," he vowed softly. "No one but you."

✤

Something woke Seregil just before dawn. As he lay there with Alec asleep beside him, the sense of happiness was even stronger, like being filled with sunlight. He'd never felt like this before. It took a moment to realize that it wasn't only his own emotions he was feeling. It was almost as if he could feel a second heartbeat under his ribs.

Alec stirred beside him, then his eyes flew open in obvious surprise. "Seregil?"

"You feel it, too?"

Alec sat up, one hand pressed to his chest, just below his throat. "What is this? I feel—you!"

Laughing, Seregil pulled Alec down into his arms, heart overflowing with shared joy. "The bond. The talímenios bond. Our spirits are joined. *Chypta Aura!* I didn't think I'd ever experience it."

"Really?"

Seregil felt a twinge of a disappointment not his own. It was a little unnerving, really. This would take some getting used to. "No, I didn't mean it that way, talí. It's just that I never dared think you and I would end up this way."

"Can you hear my thoughts?"

"No, it's not like that, but I can feel how you feel."

"Me, too."

Seregil stroked Alec's cheek. "It's beautiful."

Alec closed his eyes and nodded.

"As I understand it, the sensations probably won't be this strong all the time. But the bond will be there for as long as we love each other."

Alec snuggled closer. "I don't plan on that changing, so I guess you're stuck with me."

"Well, I can only think of one response to that."

"Oh? Oh!"

When they woke for the second time, Alec could hear the clatter of dishes and fire irons in the house beyond.

"We've missed breakfast," Seregil said with yawn.

Alec reeked of sex and his bladder was full, but suddenly the thought of facing their friends was daunting, especially in this condition.

Seregil understood without being told. Perhaps it was the bond again. "Get dressed," he whispered.

Together they climbed out the bedroom window and snuck into the unattended stable for their horses. They didn't bother with saddles, but rode bareback up to the otter pond for a swim.

It was still chilly, but Seregil stripped and dove into the water, only to come up sputtering. "Bilairy's balls, that's cold!"

A mother otter and her two pups watched them from the bank, apparently not welcoming this interruption of their morning fishing. Alec sank into the water, not finding it as bad as all that. He swam over to Seregil and wrapped his arms around him as they stood there in the chest-deep water. "You're always cold."

Seregil shivered against him, but he was smiling. "You're always warm. And as much as I'd love to make love to you again right here and now, I'm afraid your warmth is no match for frigid water."

They contented themselves with helping each other wash. Then, dressed and refreshed, they rode back to the house and sauntered into the kitchen in search of food as if they'd just been out for an early ride. Arna was there, however. She took one look at the pair of them and burst out laughing. "So you finally came to your senses, eh?"

Alec's face went hot and he was strongly tempted to turn tail and run.

But Seregil just laughed as he poured himself a cup of tea from the pot warming on the hearth. "Yes, we did. Any breakfast left?"

On the surface things were the same as they'd always been, but the looks Micum, Kari, and the servants gave him when they thought Alec wasn't looking told another story. It was embarrassing, but he didn't regret anything.

He sparred with Micum in the morning, grateful beyond words that his friend didn't bring up the subject of the night's activities, then he and Seregil helped him build a haystack in one of the fields behind the house.

The day turned warm. When Micum went back to the house to fetch them some water, Seregil pulled Alec around to the back of the stack and gave him a shove, toppling him over on his back in the crisp, fragrant hay. Grinning, Seregil straddled him and rested his hands on either side of Alec's head. "I slept very well last night, thanks to you."

"So did I, once you let me." Even after everything they'd shared last night, Alec still wasn't beyond blushing. There was more than embarrassment to it this time, though.

Seregil's grin was crooked as he took in the sudden bulge in Alec's breeches. He lowered himself slowly down to let Alec feel his own hardness.

"Here? No!" Alec gasped, trying to push him off.

"Just a taste," Seregil murmured, overwhelming his lover's protests with a kiss. Alec squirmed under him in a rather half-hearted fashion—which only made matters worse, of course—then gave in and kissed him back, tongue meeting tongue. That was still strange, but oddly intimate and exciting, too.

Lost in this soft give and take, neither of them was aware of Micum's return until he threw a flagon of cold water over them.

"Bilairy's balls!" Seregil sputtered, rolling off Alec.

"Someone else's, I'd say," Micum observed with a shrewd grin. "It's a good thing I didn't bring Illia back with me."

Alec jumped up and pulled the front of his sweat-soaked shirt down, though Micum's obvious amusement was quickly curing that problem.

Micum laughed. "Go clean up. You've got time for a wash before supper, and some more cold water will do you both good."

Seregil flipped him a rude gesture as they walked away, but he was still grinning, apparently not embarrassed in the least. Alec's face was burning and he suddenly felt a little sick.

Seregil's smile disappeared as he laid a hand on Alec's shoulder. "I'm sorry. I should have thought—"

"It's bad enough that everyone knows," Alec muttered. "They don't have to see, too."

The minute the words were out of his mouth he knew he'd hurt Seregil, even without the bond to tell him.

Still, his lover's grey eyes were kind as he said, "I understand, talí. I'm sorry. I should have realized."

That just made Alec feel worse. "It's just—"

"Still the good Dalnan?"

"After last night?" Alec made a conscious effort not to look around for people as he took Seregil's hand. In the distance he could see Illia playing some game in the kitchen yard that involved a lot of jumping.

Seregil squeezed his hand, letting him know his unspoken apology was accepted. "I don't expect you to change, Alec. I like you just the way you are."

They turned in early that night. Alec had hardly latched the door before Seregil was in his arms, kissing him deeply as he backed Alec up against the wall by the door. He buried his fingers in Seregil's still-damp hair as Seregil pressed against him, letting him feel his renewed arousal.

This time Alec didn't object. Hoping to make up for his reaction at the haystack, he pulled Seregil's shirt off over his head and licked his neck, tasting the lingering hint of salt from their day's labors.

Seregil reciprocated as he steered Alec to the bed, dragged him onto it, and flopped down on top of him. The sensation of Seregil's rising passion, coupled with his own, made him forget about worrying if anyone in the house knew what they were up to.

"Is this going to be a habit?" he asked between kisses, grabbing Seregil's backside with both hands.

Seregil raised an eyebrow at him, grin a little crooked. "I certainly hope so!"

Tata
zoisite.ru

The Summer Players

(working title)

Forthcoming from Spectra in 2011.

"My lord, it's said that there is no way to cheat at bakshi, so I can only assume you are using magic," Duke Koris growled as Seregil slapped down one of his carnelian pieces and captured the Duke's spear.

The Three Dragons gambling house stood a few doors down from the Drake and was even more opulent, attracting a clientele made up of higher ranking nobles. It was only by Reltheus' invitation that Seregil and Alec were here at all. Seregil's reputation was well known in the Street of Lights, however, and quite a crowd had gathered around the bakshi table to see him pitted against Koris, a young rake with a reputation of his own, one that had gotten him banned from several of the brothels here in the Street, including Eirual's, as it happened. Seregil was enjoying besting the man very much.

"No magic, your grace, just Illior's luck," Alec drawled, leaning on the back of Seregil's chair.

"I've played him enough myself to agree, Koris," Reltheus told the man. "He's just damn good, and lucky."

"It's all right," Seregil said, sliding another carnelian piece into place in front of Koris's lapis one to blunt the spear. Picking up the captured stones one by one, he glanced up at the duke with a cold smile. "I'm sure his Grace wasn't impugning my honor."

The duke, however, was drunk and not put off by the veiled threat. Lord Seregil was better known for avoiding duels than fighting them. "Six rounds in a row? You must have a charm on you somewhere!"

A murmur went through the crowd; it was a serious charge.

Seregil leaned back in his chair and spread his arms. "Search me, your grace. I swear by Illior you'll find nothing of the sort." He looked around at the crowd with the slightly inane grin he affected when dealing with situations like this among the nobles. "Why, the rest of you can wager on it, but I say your money is best laid on me!"

"Yes, have him strip!" one of the ladies cried, holding up her silk purse, and the cry was quickly taken up by the crowd.

Koris's smile was mean. "Yes, I'll take that wager. Fifty gold sesters says he has a luck piece or mark on him. What say you, Lord Seregil? Will you stand by your offer?"

"I suppose I must," Seregil said with a shrug.

"But how will we know it?" an older noble demanded. "A charm could be anything. Is there a wizard here?"

"Here's one!" someone at the back of the crowd shouted.

Old Reneus, one of the senior Orëska wizards, was none too pleased to be pressed into service for such a menial task, but with some cajoling and a fresh cup of wine he finally consented.

"Now you've done it," Alec muttered as Seregil handed him his sword belt and pulled off his boots and socks.

The wizard took each one with evident distaste and quickly handed them back. "No magic here."

"Better than a duel," Seregil whispered back, then climbed up onto his chair so everyone had a good view of him. "Really, your Grace, you're throwing your money away." He slipped off his coat and dropped it into Alec's waiting arms. The wizard took it and searched through the pockets. Seregil pulled off his shirt and tossed it to the man.

"There, you see? Nothing," said Seregil, turning for the crowd to inspect his lean, bare torso.

Koris smirked up at him. "There are still places to hide something. Keep going."

"Perhaps he has it hanging from his cock!" one wag suggested loudly.

"I'd like to see that," the woman who'd placed the first bet concurred. "Come on now, Lord Seregil. Out with it!"

One thing Seregil had never managed to master was blushing at will, but he made a good job of looking comically outraged. "You're not serious? Really now, your Grace, I've left those days behind me."

"A wager is a wager, my lord, unless you'd rather settle this on the plain?" said Koris.

"I'm afraid he's within his rights, Seregil," Reltheus reminded him.

Dueling was not allowed with the city, but a blind eye was turned on whatever went on outside its walls and killing someone in a formal duel was not considered murder. It had been some time since Seregil had fought for his honor.

"Very well, then." He unlaced his leather trousers and pushed them and his linen down with a graceful flourish. The crowd exploded in applause and laughter. Those closest to Alec slapped him on the back. Seregil climbed off the chair and stood grinning, hands on hips, as his trousers were inspected, then took them back and dressed as carefully as if he was in front of his looking glass at home, smoothing out every wrinkle. Money was changing hands around him and it was clear that public sentiment was on his side, for whatever reason.

Taking his place again, he raised his chin and grinned across the gaming table at his opponent. "Shall we continue, your grace?"

More applause erupted at the duke's expense.

Caught, Koris had no choice but to finish—and lose—the game. With gritted teeth his paid off the wager, swept his stones back into their fancy embroidered bag, and strode off with all the dignity he could muster.

Seregil looked around at his admirers. "Next?"

The woman who'd championed the wager took the chair Koris had vacated and poured her stones into the polished tray in front of her. They were made of blue opal, and she held one up, showing him Illior's crescent inlaid in silver on the back of it. "The Lightbringer will have to decide between us, my lord, for I've been known to have the Immortal's favor, as well. Or would you like to inspect my clothing for charms first?"

"A tempting offer, Marquise, but your honor is above reproach."

"You're very gallant, Lord Seregil, but now I'm disappointed," she said with a teasing smile. "Well, you had your chance. Shall we play?"

They were still arranging their stones for the first round when a young page made his way through the crowd and whispered something to Alec. He, in turn, leaned down and whispered in Seregil's ear, "We have to go."

Seregil quickly made his apologies to the disappointed noblewoman and the crowd and scooped up his stones.

"What is it?" he asked as they hurried out.

"I don't know, but it must be important. Kepi's outside, asking for us, and he wouldn't do that if it wasn't important, would he?"

"Most likely not."

They found the boy waiting for them on the pavement, under the watchful eye of the doorman, who clearly disapproved of such an unsightly character on the Street.

Seregil and Alec hustled him quickly out of sight into the shadows beyond the reach of the street lanterns.

"What is it?" Seregil demanded.

"That actor fellow, Atre the Mycenian? He's a friend of yours, ain't he?"

"How in the world did you know that?"

Kepi just winked and grinned.

"Yes, he's a friend of ours. What of it?"

"Well, he got hisself knifed tonight."

"Bilairy's balls! Where?" asked Seregil.

"Down at the waterfront, back of the Skulpin. I just heard of it and I come straight up to tell you. Your man at the house told me were you was."

"The Skulpin?" said Alec. "What was he doing down there?" The gambling house was just outside of the respectable commerce district of the Lower City, and catered mostly to locals and sea faring men. There were plenty of cutpurses, bawds, and footpads about at this time of night, ready to relieve the unwary of their winnings.

"Is he alive?"

"He was when my friend heard about it. I went to your house and they told me you were here. I came straight on."

"Good lad." Seregil took half a dozen coppers from his purse and gave them to the boy. Kepi made him another ill-formed bow and took off at a run, darting between horses and carriages. He was soon out of sight among the evening crowd.

They made most of the long ride down to the Lower City at a gallop and found the actor still alive and groaning on a couch in an poorly lit back room of the gambling den. He was dressed uncharacteristically plainly without a jewel on him—an apparent attempt to fit in with his surroundings, perhaps, or he'd been robbed.

A small crowd of ne'er do wells and doxies were peering in from the doorway, but parted for Alec and Seregil, who had come armed.

A drysian was with Atre, tending to a wound on his belly. The actor was white-faced and looked frightened, but at least he was conscious.

"What happened?" Seregil asked, kneeling down beside him and taking the man's hand.

"Oh, my lords!" Atre gasped, clinging to Seregil's hand with both of his, which were sticky with blood. "How did you know?"

"Never mind that. What in Bilairy's name happened to you?"

"It was a girl. She said she was hurt, and when I tried to help her—look what she did!"

"It's not as bad as all that," the drysian scoffed as he began to bandage the wound. "Hardly more than a scratch!"

"And took your purse, I suppose," said Alec. It was a common ploy among the girl cutpurses. "What are you doing alone in a place like this?"

"Oh, you know—" Atre was too pale to blush but he looked rather ashamed of himself.

Seregil gave him a knowing look.

"Got tired of the pampered nobles and came back here, looking for a bit of rougher fun?" Brader growled as he strode into the room and stood over Atre. Apparently he'd gotten word, as well.

The actor looked away, saying nothing.

"This is no place for the likes of you," the drysian scolded. "Stay up on your heights and find your fun there. I have better things to do than patch up you silly thrill seekers."

"I will, Brother. By the Maker, I will!" Atre mumbled, then looked up imploringly at Seregil. "Please, my lord, don't leave me here!"

"Of course not," Seregil assured him, then turned to Alec. "Go ask the master of the house to hire us a carriage, will you?"

"No need," said Brader. "Teibo is coming with the cart."

The drysian finished with the bandage and straightened up. "There, that should hold your guts in well enough. See that you keep the wound clean and it should be healed in a week or so, if a bit sore."

"I have to be on stage tomorrow!"

"That's why you have an understudy," Brader said, handing the healer some silver.

The drysian nodded to them and took his leave.

"Oh, Calieus will be pleased!" the young actor groaned. He'd only recently taken on the young Skalan actor. "He hangs over me like a carrion crow, just waiting for something like this to happen."

Seregil chuckled. "It's his job, isn't it? And I really don't think you can blame this on your understudy." He washed his hands with the water left in the pitcher the healer had used and stood up. "Honestly, if you'd wanted to come someplace like this, you should have asked us. We'd have come with you, and kept you out of trouble like this."

"Very kind of you, my lord, but I think my friend here should take the healer's advice," Brader said.

Just then they heard the clatter of a cart arriving. Brader lifted Atre in his arms as if he weighed no more than a child and carried him out. Old Zell had come with the boy and clucked his tongue as

Brader placed the wounded man on some folded blankets in the back of the cart.

"Really, I think a carriage would be more comfortable," said Seregil. "I'll happily pay."

"No need, my lord," Brader said gruffly. "With respect, we take care of our own." He climbed in beside Atre and Teibo snapped the reins over the glossy white mare's back and set off.

"That was a bit rude!" Alec muttered. "We might just as well have stayed at the gambling house."

"Strange sort of place for anyone who loves luxury as much as our actor friend to turn up, don't you think?" asked Seregil.

"You think he was lying about why he was down here?"

"Perhaps not, but does Atre strike you as the sort of man who would stop to help a street urchin on a dark street?"

"Not really."

Seregil gazed thoughtfully after the cart.

"So long as we're down here, I'd like to look in at that temple and see if that boy is still there," said Alec, glad to see that their horses hadn't been stolen while they were inside.

"At this hour?"

"A temple doesn't close. At least not a Dalnan one. You can go home if you want. I won't be long."

Seregil swung up into the saddle and gathered Cynril's reins. "Then I might as well tag along."

They hadn't gone far when Alec said softly, "Did you enjoy your performance back there at the Three Dragons?"

"My amazing winning streak, you mean?" Seregil said with a wink.

"No."

"Ah, the stripping naked in front of a hundred or so noblemen and women part of the evening. 'Enjoy' isn't the word I'd use, but it was satisfyingly useful."

"Useful!"

"Talí, before I met you, Lord Seregil was known for things like that. Well, not usually in such a public place, perhaps—"

"Perhaps?" Alec raised a skeptical eyebrow at that.

"At parties, mostly."

"So you did that a lot?"

"Now and then, just to keep up my reputation. Mostly it was things like getting other young nobles into trouble stealing things like public statues or bluecoats' horses while we were drunk, slumming in borrowed clothes, or daring each other to jump off Widow's Cliff into the sea. You should try that. Very invigorating—if you live."

That won him a smile and a soft laugh. "And carrying on with actors, I suppose."

"Oh, yes. And actresses."

"Am I bad for your reputation, now that we're spending so much time back in the city?"

Seregil laughed. "I'd say we dispelled any rumors of that tonight, wouldn't you? I was lucky, though."

"You did win a lot of money."

"Yes, but I was thinking more of Koris's search of my person."

Alec laughed. "What was so lucky about that? He had you standing naked on a chair."

Seregil winked at him as they passed through the glow of a street lantern. "Yes, but his search stopped short of the most obvious hiding place."

"The most—?" Alec gave him a questioning look, then realization dawned and it was replaced by one of shock. "Bilairy's balls, Seregil!"

"Close." Seregil grinned. He loved still being able to make Alec blush.

Image Gallery

The most difficult part of this book was deciding which images would go on the pages. The tremendous outpouring of fan art and the pure, overwhelming support of the fans for Lynn was amazing. This collection of short stories was an effort of love and affection from Lynn to her fans. Because of spacing issues, not all of the artwork was able to be placed in the stories they were created for still we felt it was only right that these pieces of artwork should be featured as well. The effort given by these artists—both amateur and professional—cannot be measured. Gratitude seems so inadequate as a tribute to their work.

I have never worked with someone as gracious and as caring for her fans as Lynn. I wish I could fully express to you the affection she has for her readers. Thank you for your contributions and most of all, thank you for making this book possible.

Reece Notley
Three Crow Press

Postscript: Lynn is probably one of the sweetest, coolest people in California if not the world. It was a fantastic experience to work with her and even more of a blast to share a meal or two with her.

Thank you Lynn for letting me frolic in your playground.

Seregil and Alec

Karena
Kliefoth
2010

Contributing Artists
Adriane Zonker
Angela Sopo
Anna Davidson
Anna Sommerer
Bernadette Joseco
Bettina Körner
Capucine
Casey Beck
Doug Flewelling
DragonLadyC
Franzsika Riedel
Glynnis Koike
Karena Kliefoth
Karl Engracia
Kimberly White
Tata
Kracken
Kristen Evans
Kristin McKenna
Laurel Graham
Linda Stelinski
Lindsay Mathers
Linnea Jefferson
MBP
Melissa Pritchard

Olivia Faliph
Ovsanna
Rabby
Sara Lilja
Sarah Borchart
Stela Topolcic
Tave Brandberg

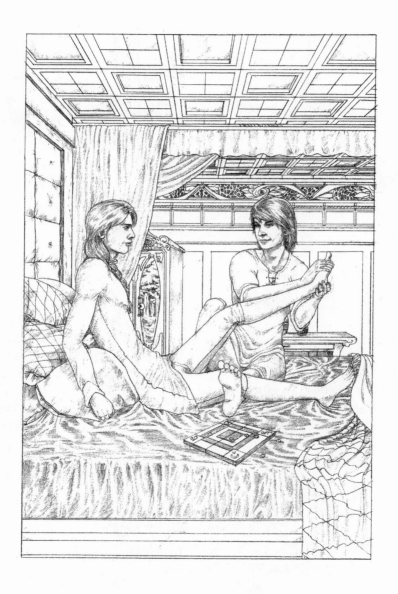

About the Author

Lynn Flewelling is best known for her internationally acclaimed Nightrunner Series and the Tamír Triad. Her first novel, *Luck in the Shadows*, was a finalist for the Compton Crook Award and made the list for Locus' 1996 Best First Novels. Since then her books have been nominated several times for the Spectrum Award and others. Her two series are published in over a dozen languages, and in audio and e-book formats. She currently lives in Redlands, California with Douglas, her husband and main muse.

Lynn's website can be found at:
http://www.sff.net/people/lynn.flewelling/

Her blog (which she updates regularly) can be found at:
http://otterdance.livejournal.com/

About the Cover Artist

As a freelance graphic artist and illustrator, Anne works for a number of print and electronic publishers along with private clients around the world. She spends her days working on projects and doodling in sketchbooks, but can sometimes be found snatching a few moments here and there for her other passions, which include writing, reading, and searching for the world's most perfect cup of hot tea.

6979447R0

Made in the USA
Lexington, KY
07 October 2010